Dragon Smoke and Magic Song

To Rebekah
and for Woody
who left early

DRAGON SMOKE AND MAGIC SONG

DAVID HARVEY

Illustrations by Pauline Baynes

George Allen & Unwin
Sydney   London   Boston

©David Harvey 1984
This book is copyright under the Berne Convention.
No reproduction without permission. All rights reserved.

First published in 1984
George Allen & Unwin Australia Pty Ltd
8 Napier Street, North Sydney NSW 2060 Australia

George Allen & Unwin (Publishers) Ltd
18 Park Lane, Hemel Hempstead,
Herts HP2 4TE England

Distributed in New Zealand by
Book Reps (New Zealand) Ltd
48 Lake Road, Northcote, Auckland

National Library of Australia
Cataloguing-in-Publication entry:

Harvey, David.
Dragon smoke and magic song.
ISBN 0 86861 425 4.
I. Title.
A823'.3

Set in 13/15pt Baskerville by BudgetSet, Australia
Printed in Hong Kong by South China Printing Co.

Contents

The Unicorns and the Giant 1
The Dragon Beneath the Stairs 17
When the Dragon Lost His Fire 30
The Watch Dragon 46
The Lord of the North Spire 67
Ngarara the Taniwha 89

The Unicorns and the Giant

One day, long, long ago, Celiphon the unicorn led the unicorns to a beautiful, pure white, sandy beach washed by the azure waters of the Western Sea to sing their songs. Throughout the morning the unicorns had frolicked and fed in the emerald meadows, drunk from the crystal streams and rested in the cool shade of the tall, spreading, leafy trees. But it was time for them to sing, and all the other animals from near and far came to the beach to hear the songs of the unicorns.

Celiphon the First Singer was the tallest, oldest and most beautiful of all the unicorns. His proud white mane drifted slightly in the cool breeze. His silver hooves glistened brilliantly and his pure white coat and feathery fetlocks shone with a gentle sheen. His ivory horn, that distinguishing mark of all unicorns, glowed in the afternoon sun. His eyes were deep and dark and kind, and as he watched the animals gather he was pleased that he and the other unicorns could bring so much pleasure and happiness with their songs.

As the animals gathered, the rippling surface of the sea was broken by the emergence from the depths of the Merepeople who are also called the High Elves of the Western Sea. The Merepeople live beneath the waves in great castles and minarets covered with multi-coloured mother-of-pearl. They can talk with the fish and the Great Whales of the deep and they ride upon the backs of the fast-moving dolphins. The Merepeople, too, had come to hear the songs of the unicorns.

When all the animals and the Merepeople were comfort able, Celiphon began to sing. One by one, all the other unicorns joined in, some singing low, some high, but all in harmony. The song was so wonderful that all who heard it felt a great peace and an incredible warmth flow over them. As the unicorns continued with their song, an air of calm

The Unicorns and the Giant

fell upon the land and the sea, the wind stopped and the waves were still and the leaves on the trees ceased to rustle. Even the smallest grasshopper scratching his legs together on a blade of grass stopped and listened, and all that could be heard was the song of the unicorns, the purest sound on all the Earth.

When the sun set, the unicorns stopped their song, and, in the pure bright light of the Evening Star which rose in the West over the sea, the animals left the beach and went to their homes. The Merepeople gave their thanks and returned to their palaces beneath the waves and the unicorns trotted gracefully over the emerald meadows to their caves in a small range of hills.

But that night was a rare and frightening one. No one, not even Celiphon, could remember a night like it. For on that night there was a storm. And what a storm it *was*! The night wind grew in strength until it was a howling gale and it chased large, black, wet clouds before it. As the clouds dashed against the hills and mountains, they released a flood of driving, pounding rain. The black clouds grew in number as they were ceaselessly driven inland. Suddenly a ghastly blue streak of lightning tore the sky in half, illuminating the land around with a pale and ghostly glare. It was followed a moment later by a deafening burst of thunder. The unicorns were safe and dry in their caves, but they could not sleep for the noise, and the unicorn foals were frightened, wondering if this could indeed be the end of the world. The adult unicorns did their best to reassure them, but even they were a little frightened. They could hear the mad pounding and roaring of the waves as they beat against the pearl-white sand of the beach and even though they were some distance from the sea, they could see the phosphorescence of the white waves, the horses of the sea. The sky was so black and cloud-enshrouded that the Evening Star was nowhere to be seen, and as the night went on and the storm mounted in its fury, it seemed as if the unicorns could hear muttering and mumbling through the thunder, and high-pitched, crazy laughter as the lightning flashed through the sky.

But the long night ended at last and, as the sun began to rise in the East, light blue sky appeared through a break in the clouds that grew larger and larger. The wind dropped and the rain stopped and the thunder, which had roared and growled above them all night, began to fade away into the distance. Slowly the sky began to clear until, within an hour or so, there was not a cloud to be seen, and the sun shone warm and merry out of a perfect sky.

The unicorns slowly left their caves, thankful that the storm was over. They expected to see a picture of ruin and destruction before them, but the grass in the emerald meadow was drying in the sun, waving happily before the light breeze that blew in from the ocean. A few leaves had blown down from the spreading shady trees that stood like patient sentinels, as if nothing had happened.

Celiphon went down to the beach. The sea was smooth, blue and calm. There was not a piece of flotsam, jetsam or seaweed to be seen. The beach was just as they had left it. Celiphon was pleased, for unicorns are very tidy beasts that cannot abide untidiness or disorder. Then, suddenly, his sharp ears picked up a strange rumbling, rasping sound. He turned and looked along the beach and his great, dark soft eyes nearly started out of his head. For there, lying on the ground where the sand met the meadow, was an enormous man, asleep and snoring. Celiphon was speechless for a moment or two. Then he trotted over to the huge figure, his silver hooves swishing in the powdery sand.

The huge man was, of course, a giant. Celiphon looked carefully at him. He had heard of giants, but had never seen one. The giant had a large, wrinkled face almost completely covered with a big, bristly, red beard. In the middle of his forehead was one enormous eye, which was shut. The giant's body was large, tough and ropy. He looked strong rather than fat and he wore a brown woolly tunic down to his knees. On his legs were thick leggings crisscrossed with leather garters. Around his waist was a great, thick belt, held together with a large bronze buckle. His arms were as large as tree trunks, his hands as big as boulders, and his fingernails were chewed and ragged and black with grime.

Celiphon knew what he had to do. The other unicorns must be told. Every animal must be told of this strange new arrival on the Western Shore. Celiphon turned and galloped like the wind towards the other unicorns who were grazing in the emerald meadows.

'There is a giant!' he cried. 'There is a giant on the beach!' The unicorns became very excited at the news. The birds flew down from the trees and listened, then flew to all points of the island to spread the word.

As the news spread, the animals stopped whatever they were doing and hurried to the Western Shore. Before long the sleeping giant was surrounded by every sort of animal, beast and bird imaginable. The animals did their best to be quiet and not disturb the giant's sleep, but there was a quiet hum of amazement as they looked at him curiously. The giant snorted and grunted and stirred, rolled onto one side and rubbed his one huge eye with his knotty fists.

'Well,' he said, and the sound of his voice was like a bass drum. 'What have we here? An island of animals?'

'Welcome, great giant,' said Celiphon politely, because unicorns were always polite, and especially to strangers and visitors. 'You are in the land Lyonessia in the Western Sea, far, far away from the Land of Men known as Acquitannia. Only animals live in this land and they all live at peace, one with another. I am Celiphon, First Singer of the unicorns. May I enquire your name?'

'My name. My name.' The giant began to laugh, and the sound of his deep rumbling laughter shook the ground. 'So, you want to know my name? Names are not cheap. Real names hold secrets where I come from. Names can be magic. But a name. Let me see.' And the giant scratched his head with his dirty fingernails and made his hair even more tangled and untidy than it had been before.

The Unicorns and the Giant

'I know,' he said. 'You can call me Yunoculis.'
And he laughed again and screwed up his face in merriment.

'It is a pleasure to meet you, Yunoculis,' said Celiphon. All the animals murmured, 'Hello Yunoculis,' in the hope that the giant would feel welcome.

'So this is Lyonessia in the Western Sea,' said the giant. 'Is this the land where dragons live?'

'Most certainly.' said Celiphon. 'And rocs, gryphons, phoenixes and manticores and many other strange and wonderful beasts. And all live happily together.'

'I have heard of this place, even from where I live,' said the giant.

'Where do you come from?' asked Celiphon.

'I am from the Land of Ice and Fire, far in the north, where in the winter the ice ships sail, and the Frost Giants breathe their frozen breath from the great lands of the trackless north to the cold isles of Ultima Thule,' replied the giant.

'I went sailing in my coracle,' he continued, 'to hunt the giant sea sturgeon, and was caught in a storm, and was blown hither and yon by wind, and tossed every which way by waves until I was thrown out of my little craft and washed upon these shores. So here I am, and I am so very, very hungry.'

'Oh, food is no problem,' said Celiphon. 'Just follow me.'

And off he cantered, with the giant following and chortling happily to himself. Celiphon led the giant to the fruit tree groves, and a little while later he returned. Yunoculis followed him, but a little more slowly this time, for cradled in his arms was a huge quantity of fruit. He sat down on the beach and ate hungrily. He had brought so much food with him that he ate well into the afternoon, and the animals were amazed, for they had never seen such an appetite. When Yunoculis had finished, he went to the crystal stream, knelt down and lapped up great gulps of water.

By this time the unicorns were ready to sing their songs. The animals gathered on the beach and Yunoculis took a seat a short distance away. The Merepeople arrived, as was their custom, and were not at all surprised to see Yunoculis. They had been well aware of his difficulties in the storm and had ordered the Great Whales to help the distressed creature from the North as he floundered in the water. Yunoculis was not aware of this, of course, and the Merepeople were too polite to tell him, for they did not wish to cast a life debt upon him.

After the unicorns had finished singing and the animals had departed, Celiphon went up to the giant, who was shaking and sobbing.

'Is anything wrong, Yunoculis?' he asked.

The giant lifted his huge head, and from his great eye flowed enormous tears.

'Those were the most beautiful songs that I have heard. Were they songs of welcome?'

'Oh, no,' said the unicorn, and laughed merrily. 'It is something we do every afternoon. For the gift of the

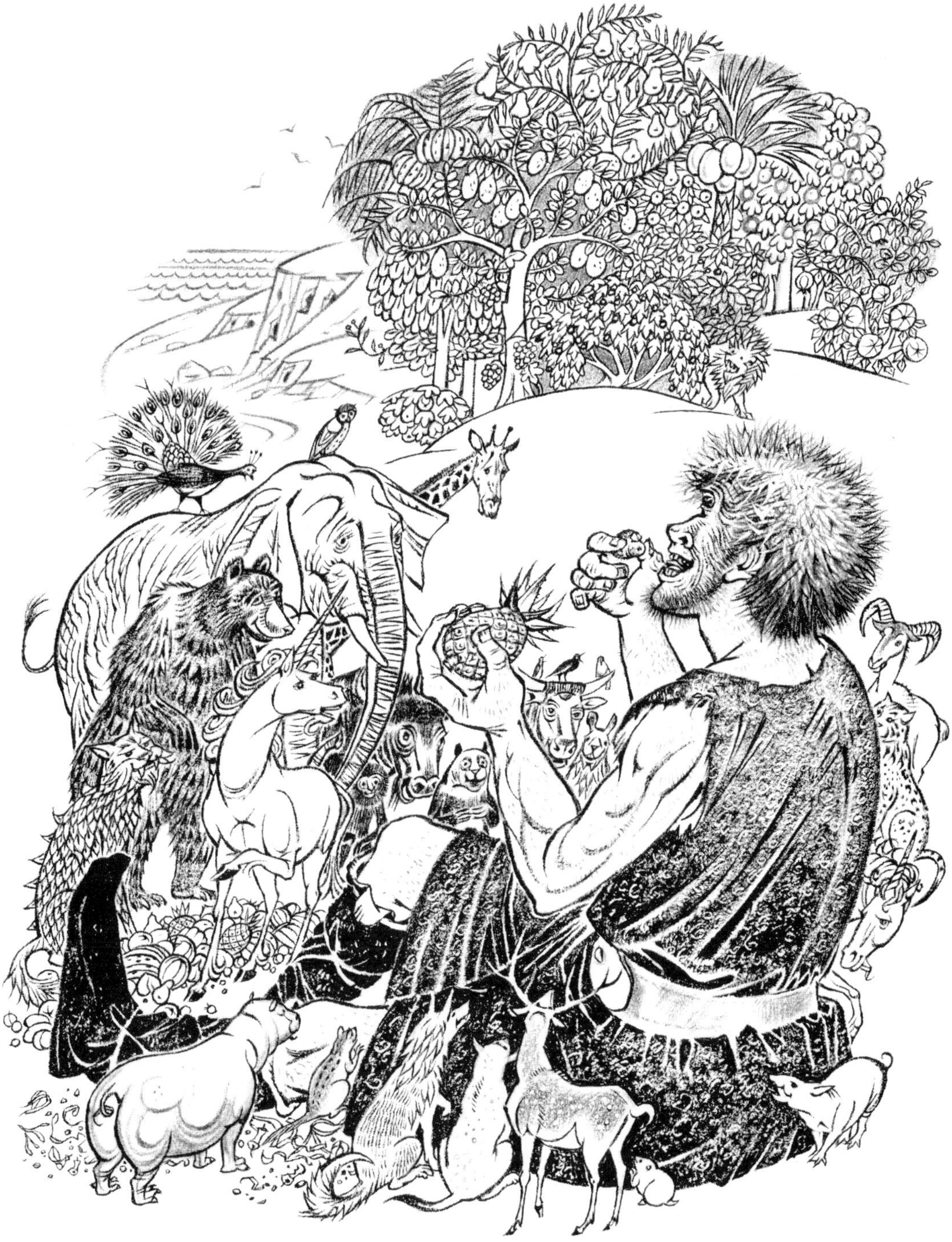

unicorns is the gift of song. It is a gift we are happy to share with others, and bring them joy.'

'My land is harsh and cold,' said Yunoculis, 'and we have little time for song. Most of our time is spent hunting for food. Our bards chant sagas of our history and heroes in our halls in the long winter nights, but their songs have not the beauty of yours.'

'I am glad you liked our songs, Yunoculis,' said the Unicorn. 'Please feel free to listen to them for as long as you like. It is our pleasure to sing.'

'Thank you, Celiphon,' replied the giant, 'and now, if you will excuse me, I must get some sleep.'

Yunoculis lay down. In a moment he was asleep and snoring loudly. Celiphon walked up the beach and towards the meadow. In the air was a curious odour he had not smelled before. But he was tired with the excitement of the day, and didn't think about it any more.

Each day Yunoculis went to the fruit tree groves, returned to the beach with his arms laden with fruit and ate noisily and long, and each afternoon he listened to the songs of the unicorns and marvelled at their beauty. But after a week, the unicorns and and the other animals noticed that something was very wrong indeed. The smell that Celiphon had noticed on the night that the giant arrived became more and more powerful and unpleasant. The animals sat further away from the unicorns than they usually did. On one dreadful day, one of the younger unicorns was so distracted and revolted by the smell that

The Unicorns and the Giant

he did not pay attention to the song and sang out of tune. This was dreadful, for it had never happened before. The young unicorn apologised profusely, but the next day the animals as well as the Merepeople sat further away, and more unicorns sang out of tune. And it was all because of the horrible smell which was daily getting worse.

That evening Celiphon stayed at the beach and thought very carefully. He sniffed around and noticed that the smell was strongest in the area where Yunoculis ate his fruit. Then it dawned on him that Yunoculis had not cleaned up after any of his meals. On the powdery sands were scattered the rinds, skins, peels and leftovers of every feast of fruit that the giant had eaten. And they were rotting. The smell was that of rotting fruit. To make matters worse, the giant had not washed since his arrival in Lyonessia. He was messy, dirty, untidy and altogether rather unpleasant to be near. That was why the unicorns were singing out of tune and why the animals were moving away.

The next day the unicorns gathered upon the beach to sing their songs, but no one came. The animals did not appear and the Merepeople remained in their palaces under the sea. The only person who came was Yunoculis, who waited for the songs to begin. But the unicorns were heartbroken. They were so sad that they could not even begin to sing, hanging their proud and beautiful heads in sorrow and shame. Yunoculis waited silently, but he did not hear the song. Rather, he heard the sobbing of the unicorns. What a sorrowful sound that was. Tears welled up from their dark, warm, kind eyes and fell like rain upon the soft sand of the beach. One by one they left the beach and, for the first time in history, the song of the unicorns was not heard on the Western Shores of Lyonessia.

Celiphon was distraught. He could not sleep for the disgrace that had come upon the unicorns. Unicorns were meant to sing; they were meant to bring joy and happiness to others. That was the purpose of their gift. If they could not sing, what could they do? Celiphon thought long and hard, and the next morning he went down to the beach.

'Good morning, Celiphon,' rumbled the giant as the unicorn approached.

'Good morning, Yunoculis,' replied Celiphon.

They stood in silence for a moment. Although Celiphon knew what he had to do, he was unsure how to start.

The giant spoke. 'I, er . . . that is to say . . . well, it's just that . . . ah . . . I like your songs so much, and I have missed hearing them since yesterday.'

'We have missed singing them,' replied Celiphon.

'Have you, really?' asked the giant.

'Yes.'

'Oh, dear,' said the giant, and he was silent for a few moments. Then he said, 'I would so like to hear your songs again. Just a little song; it needn't be a long one, but a short, beautiful song to make me feel a bit better.' The giant's words flowed out like a torrent.

'I'm sorry, Yunoculis, but we can't,' said Celiphon.

'Can't! Can't!' shouted the giant, becoming impatient,

The Unicorns and the Giant

for he could sense that he was getting nowhere and was beginning to feel embarassed. 'Why on earth not?'

Celiphon became wary. The giant was very big, and it was plain he was getting angry. Who knew what he might do if he lost his temper? Celiphon chose his words with care.

'There is a problem,' he said. 'Not a big problem, or it may not be so to you, but it is for us, and for those who come to listen to us.'

'Oh?' said the giant. 'And, tell me, what might this problem be?'

'Where you come from, your ways are different. In the Land of Ice and Fire it may be all right to leave things where they lie, but here we like things neat and tidy and clean. The rinds and leftovers from your meals make the most frightful smell. The animals don't like it and won't come to listen, and we have found the smell so distracting that we cannot concentrate on our song.'

'Is that so?' shouted the giant angrily. 'Just who do you think you are, telling me I am a messer and a smelly fellow? Leave me, unicorn! I don't care if I never hear another of your songs again. I did very well without them before I came here, and I can do without them again.'

And he stamped off, making the ground shake. Celiphon walked miserably to the caves. He had failed.

But that night, as the giant sat on the beach in the midst of his smelly squalor, looking out over the moonlit sea, he realised that he really did miss the song of the unicorns, and he did want to hear it again. Perhaps he was being a little selfish, and perhaps he should respect the ways of the land in which he was a welcome guest. He didn't really want to be lonely.

After thinking all night, next morning he busied himself on the beach instead of going to the fruit tree groves. First, he gathered up all his mess, the rinds, the skins, the peels, the pips, the stones, the cores and all the little bits and pieces and crumbs and stacked them into a huge pile. Then with his great, horny hands he dug a deep hole. It was so deep that when he stood in it he couldn't see over the top. Then he got out of the hole, shovelled all the litter into it and covered it up. He took a great feathery palm frond and swept and smoothed the beach until it was spick and span, and every grain of sand glittered in the sunlight.

After he had finished he was so hot that he decided to go for a swim. He went to the cool, clear, crystal stream, took off all his clothes and plunged in. He took some large pumice stones from the shore and scrubbed and scoured his enormous body until it was free of every speck of grime. He washed his clothes and rubbed them with sand and pumice. And when he had finished, he brushed his hair and beard until all the knots and tangles were out. He got dressed and looked at his reflection in the crystal stream, and he couldn't recognise himself. Then he set off across the emerald meadow to the caves in the hills.

The unicorns saw him coming from afar, but didn't recognise him. The only familiar thing about this giant was

The Unicorns and the Giant

the huge eye in the middle of his scrubbed and rosy forehead. This was very strange. All the unicorns stared at him, and gradually, one by one, they recognised him.

Yunoculis walked up to Celiphon.

'I must apologise,' said the giant. 'I have been messy and ill-mannered and I have tried to make amends. I should like you to come to the beach and see what I have done.'

And so the unicorns went to the beach, led by Yunoculis the giant. When they got there, they couldn't believe their eyes. In front of them was the neatest, tidiest, cleanest beach they had ever seen. It was better than before. The unicorns whinnied for pleasure and dashed out onto the sand.

'I thought about what you said,' Yunoculis told Celiphon, 'and you were right. It was wrong of me to leave a mess on the beach and spoil everyone's pleasure. It was bad and selfish.'

'Think no more of it,' said Celiphon happily. 'For on this beach we shall be able to sing better than ever.'

He walked on to the beach, and began to sing. The other unicorns stopped their play and came over to him, and one by one joined in. They sang a song of joy and happiness that was so beautiful and wonderful that Yunoculis sat down in amazement. The song wafted out over the land and the water, and although it was morning, animals and Merepeople gathered around the Western Shore, delighted that the unicorns were singing again.

Dragon Smoke and Magic Song

What joy there was on the day that the unicorns sang after their sadness and their silence! The song they sang was greater, stronger, more intricate, more wondrous and more beautiful than any ever sung by any unicorn. Long into the afternoon they sang, and Celiphon wove more and more musical webs into the theme, and the world stood still, for it was enraptured. Then, as the sun began to set in the evening sky and the silver ship of the Evening Star sailed into the heavens, a new and different sound could be heard, a deep sound that was mellow and rich, and in harmony with the song of the unicorns, yet that added a quality to the song that had never been heard before. It was the magnificent bass voice of Yunoculis the giant, who, unable to restrain himself, had decided to join in. But no one took offence, for Yunoculis was in harmony not only with the unicorns, but with everything in Lyonessia. And now, when the unicorns sing, they are joined by the great giant, who will sing with them for evermore.

The Dragon Beneath the Stairs

Igniferox, the great bronze dragon, had been sitting in his cave for three weeks, waiting and watching. In the rocky nest before him were three eggs. Igniferox was pleased, and he hummed to his eggs with a deep rumbling hum that sounded like thunder on the horizon. For Igniferox was the most powerful of his race, though for a dragon he was very young, being only one thousand, one hundred and five years old. Dragons, of course, live forever and grow in size, strength and power as long as they are needed, and Igniferox was the most needed dragon on Dragon Island. His breath was so hot that it could melt the icebergs that drifted down from the north. Snowflakes became gentle rain before his flames, rain to nourish the fabulous scarlet orchids that grew in profusion in the lush forests of Dragon Island.

Suddenly the eggs began to rock in the dragon nest, and, with a loud crack, began to open. Wild with joy, Igniferox went to the mouth of his cave, and, with a mighty roar, launched himself into the sky, opening his eighteen-metre-wide wings. As the air struck them, there came a sound like the boom of a cannon. Three eggs, he thought; one bronze, one gold, one green. Three colours out of the same clutch. He circled higher and higher through the warm morning mists that shrouded the great mountain peak of Dragon Island. The other dragons heard his roar and the rushing wind as his wings beat majestically in the air, and with answering cries they left their caves and joined him in his celebration until the sky around the summit of the great mountain was full of dragons glinting and glistening in the morning sun, the light flashing gold and green and bronze off their gleaming scales.

Igniferox returned to his cave and the dragon nest. There, as he expected, was a small bronze dragon about a metre long, stretching and drying his miniature wings. And

The Dragon Beneath the Stairs

there, crawling out of the nest was the gold one, already puffing smoke as she panted with the unaccustomed effort of movement. But what was this? In the middle of the dragon nest, squeaking a squeak that in time would mature into an earth-shattering roar was – a red dragon!

A red dragon: oh, the shame of it! Never before had there been a red dragon. No one had red dragons. They were unheard of, undreamed of. He, Igniferox Major, mighty protector of the skies, had a freak in his nest. And a small freak, at that; this red thing was only thirty centimetres long. *Still,* thought the great bronze dragon, *he is well formed and his wings are large and complete. He should be a good flier.*

But these comforting thoughts were thrust to one side as Igniferox wrestled with the real problem. There was a freak in the nest. A great tear of shame welled up in his golden eye and trickled down his scaly cheek, falling with a great splash on the head of the red dragon. Igniferox hung his head in shame and stumbled out to the mouth of his cave, where he sat despondently, his wings covering his eyes.

The other dragons saw his distress, but being polite, as dragons are, they preferred not to intrude. Only when the three hatchlings emerged from the cave a week later for their first flight did the dragon community realise the reason for the shame of the great bronze. How the young, ill-mannered ones laughed! 'What is this?' they said contemptuously. 'Is this a dragon? He is so small, he must be given a name.' So, out of derision for his size, they called the red dragon Minimus, meaning 'smallest', and flew away, laughing their booming laughs which echoed off the great mountain.

The cruel naming was even more painful for Igniferox than the red dragon's birth had been. For weeks he and Minimus bore the taunts and jibes of the young dragons, and the little red dragon soon came to understand that all was not well, and that, worse still, he was the one responsible. He did not realise that his colour was an accident of birth, and that he had no control over it or over his size. But it is the doom of the young to try and change the unchangeable or take upon themselves the responsibility of doing what they in their innocence think to be right, and so one night when all was quiet and the other dragons were asleep, Minimus left the cave and launched himself out into the night sky, flying towards the stars. He knew that there was a world outside, full of adventure and wonder, a world of which his father had spoken, full of strange and amazing things and filled with creatures who walked on two legs and were called 'people'. He knew that he had to be careful of people, for they alone could destroy a dragon. He had been told on his first day out of the nest to beware particularly of people named George, who fought and killed dragons. And the other most important thing was that when he was flying he had to be especially careful of going too close to the Evening Star, the great silver ship that sailed across the sky.

Minimus stopped flying and hovered in the chill night air. Frost was gathering on his wings, but a short puff of

The Dragon Beneath the Stairs

dragon breath turned it to warm water. To the West was the Evening Star; to the South, a cross of stars. To the North was Polaris, but in that part of the sky were bears and it was not dragon territory. To the East was Orion the Hunter, waving his warning club. Minimus decided to go south. He beat his wings and surged southward through the night.

For hours he sped on; the farther he flew, the more fatigued he became. He began to forget important things, such as the first rule of flying, which is: watch the weather. He didn't see the black thunderheads forming below him, rising up at hundreds of metres a minute. He was so tired that the first huge clap of thunder nearly shocked him out of his scales. Then it was a battle as the storm winds blew and howled, and the lightning flashed stark against the dark clouds and the thunder growled like a thousand angry dragons. It was all he could do to fly, as he was tossed and buffeted by the winds and drenched by the driving rain.

At last he gained control and began to head down, down, like a red bullet. He flashed past the clouds, all tiredness gone, racing the lightning and winning, flying like a dragon, King of the Skies, in control, more powerful than the storm, a stormrider, dashing through the clouds, using the wind and the rain and the gusting gales to obtain the greatest speed. Down he flew, roaring his defiance at the storm, spreading his crimson wings, challenging the winds to take him.

Then suddenly he was through the clouds, heading for

an enormous concrete spear topped with a red light. Miraculously he swerved and missed it, but was unable to correct and rolled and tumbled through the air until he bumped and thumped and stopped outside the open door of a two-storeyed white house. Through the open door the light inside looked warm and inviting. The cold wind was blowing, and the rain had soaked his scales. Just inside the door was a huge dog, larger than Minimus, asleep and breathing heavily and regularly. Gently, quietly, he crept past the dog and into the house. From the garage next door, a strange and curious black cat blinked her eyes in disbelief. Big dogs were one thing; red dragons were impossible. She swished her tail in annoyance, but Minimus didn't know about the cat, and if he had known he wouldn't have cared. He was more intent upon warmth and shelter. As he crept into the house, he saw a perfect spot, a cupboard leading into a little room underneath the stairs. With a great sigh he heaved his aching body into the cupboard, closed the door after him, wrapped himself in a large piece of green paper and went thankfully to sleep.

For three days and nights he hung between sleep and wakefulness. At times he could hear voices, the sound of footsteps past the cupboard, the rattling of dishes or the barking of a dog. But the sound that attracted him most was the voice of a little girl.

On the third day, when the house was silent, he came out of the cupboard, refreshed and relaxed, to explore. He went along a hall, and saw a room with a tree growing in

The Dragon Beneath the Stairs

it, all covered with silver and tinsel. He went upstairs and saw a room with bookcases filled with books about dragons. *This must be the little girl's room* he thought, and considered that she would be a nice person to know. But he began to grow slightly nervous and decided to hide, not in the cupboard under the stairs but under the little girl's bed.

That night, when the little girl went to bed and after she had read a Christmas story about Santa Claus, she gathered her toy dogs about her, kissed her parents goodnight and closed her eyes as her father turned the lights out.

'Is there really a Santa Claus?' she asked.

'Wait and see in the morning,' he replied.

Minimus, who was still under the bed, had listened to the story about Santa Claus and how he flew through the air. But Santa was neither a bird nor a dragon, so how could this be? Later that night, when all was quiet and the lights were out, Minimus stealthily crept outside. The great dog was asleep, dreaming dog dreams of bones and heroes and the First Fire. The strange and curious cat was peering over the fence, unable to mind its own business. When she saw Minimus open his crimson wings and beat them against he air with a crack like a rifle shot, she had a terrible fright and ran away under the house.

Minimus headed up into the sky until he saw the city below him, gleaming and twinkling like a casket of jewels. He thought that if he flew high enough he might see Santa as he approached the city. After all, a sleigh pulled by eight reindeer led by one with a shining red nose would be difficult to miss. Minimus started a search pattern, crisscrossing the sky, but no sign did he see of Santa, sleigh or reindeer. Above him was the high cloud, freezing cold and rarely moving, but below the sky was clear. Minimus looked for an opening in the cloud above him and broke through. Above him the sky was clear and full of stars. Below him was the white expanse of white cloud, and — what was this? Sitting on a cloud was a sleigh and standing in front of it were eight reindeer. Beside the sleigh was a little old man with a white beard, wearing a rich red suit obviously designed to keep out the cold. He was sitting glumly on the cloud. *That must be Santa Claus*, thought Minimus, and gently landed on the cloud beside the sleigh.

'Are you Santa Claus?' he asked, politely extending a claw in friendly greeting.

'Yes, I suppose I am,' said the old man with a sigh, 'but I think I'll be out of a job after this. I can't move the sleigh. The runners have frozen solid to the cloud. I'd stopped to give the deer a rest before we headed down to the city to drop off all the goodies to the children, and look what happened. Stuck fast.'

'Can't the reindeer pull you off the cloud?' asked Minimus, trying to be helpful.

'No,' said Santa. 'They're tired out, and we have the whole night's flight ahead of us. We just won't be able to make it. None of the children will get any of the toys they want, and they won't believe in me any more, so I'll just

The Dragon Beneath the Stairs

fade away with the sleigh and the reindeer. No one will need me any more.'

'I know how you feel,' said Minimus. 'Dragons need to be needed. Take my father, Igniferox.'

'Igniferox?' queried Santa. 'What sort of name is that?'

'It means "fierce fire",' said Minimus. 'Now my father, he was needed to melt the icebergs and keep the frost and snow off the magic orchids.'

'Quite right,' said Santa. 'And we need him now. He could melt us out.'

Minimus had an idea.

'Santa,' he said, 'perhaps I can help. Perhaps I can melt the ice.'

'What, you?' said Santa. 'You're not big enough to melt a cloud of this size.'

'I didn't mean the cloud,' replied the dragon. 'I meant the ice around the runners of the sleigh.'

He began to grumble, as dragons do when they are building up fire pressure. Smoke poured from his dragon nostrils as he approached the sleigh.

'Careful,' cried Santa. 'Watch the wrapping paper on the presents!'

Minimus nodded to show he understood, and, with a roar, he let fly a burst of white flame from his mouth at the runners of the sleigh. Instantly the ice began to melt.

'Get aboard the sleigh!' he shouted, building up a fresh head of pressure and smoking out his ears, which is what happens if you talk and breathe fire at the same time. Santa

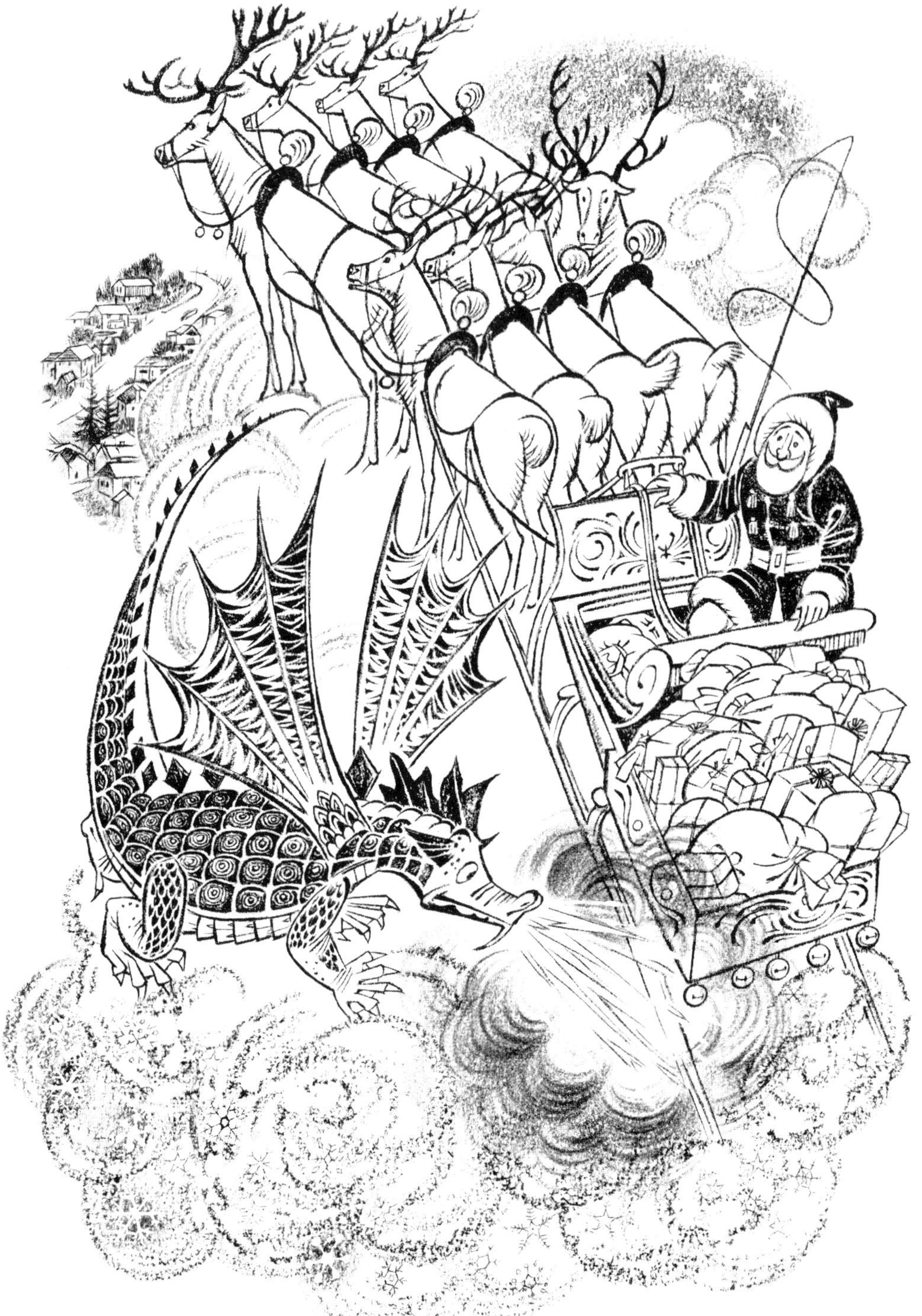

leapt to the driving seat, whip at the ready. The reindeer tensed, ready to leap upon command and hurtle skywards.

'The runners are made of metal,' Minimus spluttered. 'They will retain the heat and keep the melting process going. When I breathe, get the deer to pull.'

Immediately Minimus let fly with another enormous fireball of white flame, searing the snow and ice around the runners of the sleigh. The deer heaved and Santa shouted encouragement. With a grinding crack, the sleigh pulled free and soared aloft. Minimus roared in encouragement and flew up beside the sleigh. 'There is a little girl who isn't sure about Santa,' he said, 'and I think you should visit her house first.'

'Righto,' said Santa. 'Lead the way.'

So Minimus folded his wings and plummeted towards the city, followed closely by the reindeer and the sleigh, Santa crying, 'Tally Ho!' all the way down. Minimus led Santa to the two-storeyed white house and waited on the roof by the chimney and talked with Rudolph, Dasher and Dancer about the finer points of flying, while the merry old fellow scrambled down the chimney pot. They could hear him chuckling and chortling from the inside of the house. A little while later, Santa's red face popped out of the chimney pot.

'Onwards!' he cried. 'We have work to do!'

And so the unlikely combination of reindeer, sleigh, Santa and dragon flew once around the world, chasing the night, delivering presents and bringing happiness to all children. At the end of it, Santa stopped and pointed to the sky.

'Well, that was a good night's work. Now I must take the third star on the right and go straight on until morning and then I shall be home. You look as if you could do with the rest, too. Why don't you come along?'

'No, thank you, Santa,' said the red dragon. 'I think I should like to go back to the two-storeyed white house and see what happens there.'

And so they parted, Santa and the dragon, promising to meet on the Christmas Eve of the following year. With the dragon nearby, Santa would never get stuck again, and Minimus felt needed, at least for one night of the year.

Back he flew, racing the rays of the morning sun, and arrived at the white house just as dawn was breaking. The great dog was asleep by the doorway, peacefully dreaming the dreams that dogs dream at dawn and the black cat was nowhere to be seen. But instead of going back to the cupboard beneath the stairs, Minimus padded softly into the lounge room and hid behind the large decorated Christmas tree. He could see all the beautifully wrapped presents that Santa had left. He meant to stay awake so that he could see the happiness on the face of the little girl when she saw all the gifts, but he was so tired after all his activity of the night before that he fell fast asleep.

And he didn't hear the soft footsteps of the little girl as she came down the stairs, and he didn't know that her favourite colour was red, and that he was the first thing

The Dragon Beneath the Stairs

that she saw, although he was behind the branches and tinsel of the tree. He awoke, feeling her arms around his neck and feeling her shower kisses on his soft ears. He heard her say, 'There is a Santa — there is, there is — and he has brought me a real live dragon for my very own.'

At that moment, Minimus knew that he would never be lonely again.

When the Dragon Lost His Fire

The summer days were long and hot, and the nights were still and humid. There had been no rain for weeks; the grass was turning brown and the colourful flowers in the gardens were wilting and drooping more and more each day. People were not allowed to water their gardens or fill their swimming pools. The ground became hard and began to crack. Every day, when the sun rose, there was not a cloud in the sky, and when the sun set the sky was still clear, although it was coloured a rich orange, promising that the next day would bring more of the same.

Even Minimus, the little red dragon, was beginning to find the heat too much for him. It was certainly too hot to breathe fire, and in the afternoons he tried to keep himself cool by flapping his wings to make a light breeze that would drift over his scales and keep his body cool. The great stripy dog who lived in the white two-storeyed house would spend the day moving from one shady spot to another as the sun cast its shadows over the ground. It was too hot for him to run around and play; all he could do was sit in the shade and pant thirstily. The strange and wonderful black cat was nowhere to be seen. She had thick, black fur and found the heat unbearable. Minimus thought she must have gone under a house so that she could stay in the shade all the time.

One bright, sunny, hot morning the little girl called Leah who looked after Minimus said to him, 'Minimus, we are going to the beach for a swim. It will be nice and cool. Would you like to come?'

Minimus had never been to a beach before. He was a flying dragon and was not at all like his great cousins, the sea dragons, who lived in the ocean and rarely, if ever, came to land. But he thought it would be nice to go to a beach, especially if it was cool, and besides, it would be something new, and it could be exciting. So he nodded his head and watched as Leah began to pack towels and a picnic basket and swimming things into the car.

Then he heard Leah ask her mother, 'Can we take the dog to the beach? He is so hot and tired. He might like it.'

'No, dear,' said her mother. 'Dogs aren't allowed on the beach. He will have to stay at home. Make sure he has plenty of water so he won't get thirsty while we are away.'

Minimus stood by the car and watched as Leah filled the dog's drinking dish with fresh, cool water, led the great stripy dog into his run, and shut and locked the door. The dog pushed his black nose up to the railings of the gate, fretting that he was not allowed to go out and join the fun.

Leah and her parents put Minimus into the back seat of the car, got in themselves and drove off, heading for the beach. They decided to go to a beach on the western side of the city, big and large and open with plenty of room and large, cool, refreshing surf waves.

On the way Leah said to her father, 'Dad, if dogs aren't allowed on the beach, do you think Minimus will be allowed to go there?'

'Of course!' said her father. 'Minimus isn't a dog; he's a dragon. The rules say that only dogs and horses aren't meant to be on the beach. Since Minimus is neither a dog nor a horse, he must be allowed.'

Minimus felt very pleased with himself, curled up in the back seat of the car and went to sleep. He slept so soundly that he missed the journey to the beach across the dry and dusty roads that passed through the dry bush that was beginning to turn brown through lack of rain. He didn't wake up until the car had stopped and the first thing he heard was a muffled, swishing roar he had never heard before.

'Come on Minimus,' said Leah. 'We're here at the beach. Come and look.'

Minimus uncurled himself, hopped out of the car and padded up a sand dune covered with long, thin spinifex bushes. In front of him was an enormous beach of black sand, and beyond that was a vast expanse of water with huge waves that pounded and frothed and swished up the beach. He thought that the white crests of the waves looked like the manes of unicorns that he had been told lived on the islands of Lyonessia, but he could not see manes or horns or hooves, so he though they must have been the manes of white seahorses. The more he looked at them, the more he wanted to join them in the water and play with them. His feet began to feel very hot, even thought his feet scales were very thick. The sand was extremely hot from the beating, relentless sun. Leah's mother and father had gone down to the beach, had put up a large, colourful sun umbrella and had laid out towels and rugs on the sand. Minimus and Leah hurried down to join them. A light wind blew tufts of spinifex along the sand and was a little cooler, but not cool enough.

Leah said to Minimus, 'Come on, Minimus, let's go for a swim. It will be nice and cool.'

Minimus, who had been lying on the sand, had small

grains of sand under his scales, and they were irritating him. A swim might serve two purposes, he thought, get rid of the itches and cool me down. But he wasn't too sure. The water and the breakers looked wet and wild and — well — different. As Leah ran down to the edge of the water, Minimus followed cautiously behind her. He finally came to a halt just above the line where the breakers stopped, where the sand was wet but the water did not pound in.

By this time Leah was well out in the water, tackling the breakers and diving under them. 'Come on, Minimus!' she cried. 'There is nothing to be afraid of!'

Minimus extended one dragon claw very carefully in front of him and put it into the water. It felt cool and refreshing on his scales, and he could see the small grains of sand swirl out from under his skin and float away in the water. It really wasn't bad. In fact, it was rather nice; a dragon could have a lot of fun in the water. And so he

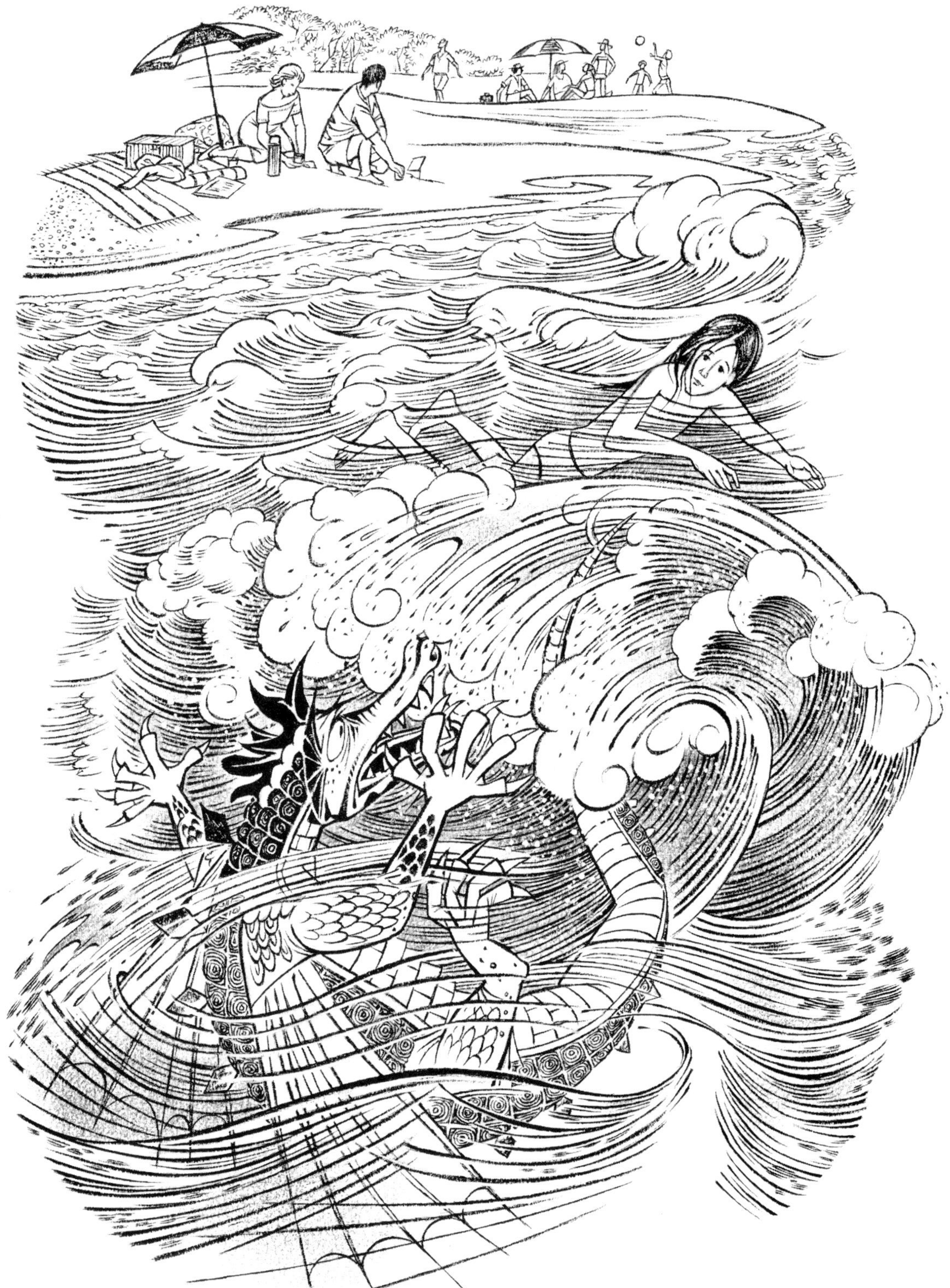

scampered in, flapping his wings, and, half leaping and half flying, cleared the first line of breakers. That was his first mistake. When he came down on the other side the water was deeper than he thought, and because dragons have short legs, he could not touch the bottom. He splashed and floundered and flapped his wings and was able to keep his head above the surface.

He opened his mouth to cry out a dragon call of distress. That was his second and biggest mistake, because he didn't see the foamy crest of another breaker bearing down on him. The next thing he knew was that the white water had gone straight into his mouth, and the wave tumbled him over and under and under and over, and he was left, high but definitely not dry, on the sand.

Poor Minimus. What a sorry and bedraggled sight he was! His scales were saturated, his wings hung down, waterlogged, his crest drooped over one eye. He felt thoroughly sad and very disenchanted with the idea of swimming. Slowly and squelchily he walked back up the beach to the umbrella and sat down in a red, dejected heap. Leah came up to him because she had seen all that had happened, but was unable to do anything to help him. She put her arms around his neck and tried to comfort him.

When the Dragon Lost His Fire

Minimus felt a little better, but was very wet and rather cold. He decided to warm himself up with a burst of flame — not a big, monstrous burst, but just enough of a puff to take the edge off the cold and damp. He opened his mouth and blew, but all that came out of his mouth was a limp puff, not of smoke, but of steam. He was puzzled and breathed in long and deep. He gurgled down in his stomach in the way dragons do before they breathe fire, and he breathed out. But there was nothing.

Minimus had lost his fire! He tried to think what could have happened, and then it dawned on him. The water! The water he had swallowed had put his fire out. What was worse, he didn't know of any cure. His father, the powerful Igniferox Major, would have known what to do, but he was far, far away on Dragon Island and could not help. Minimus was on his own, and would have to find his own fire.

Leah was very upset and she began to cry. Her mother tried to comfort her, and her father, whom she thought was meant to know everything, didn't have any answers. As they sat on the beach, wondering what they could do, a shadow fell across them. They all looked up, and saw a tall man standing beside the umbrella, wearing a brown pair of shorts and a brown shirt with a shoulder flash that read 'Dog Ranger'.

'Excuse me sir, madam,' he said, 'but I must tell you that dogs are not allowed on the beach.'

'He's no dog,' said Leah between her sobs. 'He's a dragon and my dad says that there is nothing to stop a dragon being on the beach.'

'Is that so?' said the dog ranger, and he smiled a little smile, because he had never heard that excuse before. 'If he is a dragon, let's see him breathe fire or something. I've heard that dragons breathe fire, and if he's a dragon he ought to be able to do that.'

'Come on, Minimus,' said Leah. 'Try to breathe some fire.'

Minimus tried as hard as he could, but it was no use. The water had put his fire out and there was nothing he could do to start it up again.

Leah had an idea. She said to the dog ranger, 'Dragons can fly and dogs can't. If Minimus can fly, will you let him stay on the beach?'

The dog ranger thought for a moment. 'Yes,' he said. 'If he can fly he is no dog, so he can stay.'

Minimus stood up and placed his legs in the takeoff position. He lifted his wings so they would catch the breeze, but they were heavy and wet and were still waterlogged. He tried a running start and pounded along the beach, trying to get his wings in position so he could do a glide takeoff, but he stepped on a piece of wet seaweed and fell flat on his dragon nose.

'Nice try,' said the dog ranger, 'but not good enough. Now, I have been more than patient with all this dragon talk, but enough is enough. That thing, whatever it is, can't breathe fire and it can't fly, so it can't be a dragon. It

When the Dragon Lost His Fire

doesn't purr or say "meow" so it can't be a cat. But it does have four legs and it looks to me like a dog, and that is that. You will have to get him off the beach!'

Leah's parents tried to reason with the dog ranger, but he would not be shifted from his opinion. They decided they would all go rather than let the dejected and humiliated Minimus sit in an uncomfortably hot car for the day. They packed their things up and Leah heard her father mumble some words that sounded like 'officious bureaucrats' towards the dog ranger, who was walking away down the beach.

When everything was packed in the car, they began the long, sad, silent drive home.

The great stripy dog was asleep in the sun, and was very surprised to see the family and Minimus home so early. But he was totally amazed to see Minimus with bedraggled wings, and he knew that something was wrong. As the family unpacked the car and went inside for a cup of tea, the dog tried to comfort Minimus in the way that animals do for one another, and licked the salty tears that were trickling down Minimus' scaly face. Minimus and the dog talked to one another, not in words or by moving lips, but by special movements of the body, ears, eyes and tail. In a matter of moments, the dog knew what was wrong. But old and wise and smart though he was, there was nothing he could do to bring back Minimus' fire. He did tell Minimus to lie on the hot concrete and spread his wings out so that they could dry. Minimus did so and immediately fell fast asleep. The dog sat beside him, hoping the warmth of the sun would give the power of flight back to the sad red dragon.

At sunset, Minimus awoke and felt much better and very refreshed. He stood up and stretched; his wings were dry and he flexed them proudly. With a snap and a crack like a rifle shot, he took off into the orange sky, soaring up and up in circles. He could fly, he could fly! His wings were dry and strong again.

Now for the final test. High above the city, with the red sun sinking behind the hills into the sea, he drew a deep breath and exhaled. But — nothing happened. His fire was still out and he didn't know what to do to get it back again. *What use is a dragon without fire?* he thought. *Worse than a worm.* Sadly, Minimus glided back to the two-storeyed house, padded inside and crawled into the cupboard under the stairs, where he sobbed and sobbed.

All next day, Minimus was inconsolable. Nothing Leah or her parents could do would make the little red dragon cheer up. He could not be enticed from his cupboard beneath the stairs. he would not come out to eat or drink, and remained there, curled up in a red, miserable ball.

As the day passed, Leah, too, became miserable. She wandered around the house with the corners of her mouth turned down, and every now and again large tears welled up in her eyes. Of course this had its effect upon her mother and father, who did not like to see their little girl sad for any reason. As the evening of this long, hot, sad day approached, Leah's father suggested that they all go out to dinner at a restaurant, hoping that this would make Leah and perhaps Minimus feel a little happier.

When Minimus was told that they were going out, he wearily raised his head, slowly padded out of the cupboard and went to the open door of the car. 'At least he wants to do something,' said Leah hopefully, trying to convince herself that her dragon was feeling better.

They all drove to a little restaurant that served Mexican food and was run by a man called Pepito. But when they arrived, the dining room was empty, and there were no delicious cooking smells. They all sat down at a table (Minimus curled up on a chair) and waited for someone to come and find out what they wanted to eat. They waited for a very long time; so long, in fact that Leah and Minimus were becoming restless. Even Minimus, despite his sadness and despair, was feeling extremely hungry.

Finally Leah could bear it no longer. All this sitting still was making her bored. She got up from the table and decided to look around. Minimus went with her. Before long they found the door to the kitchen. Slowly Leah pushed it open and they went in. Sitting in the middle of the kitchen, surrounded by uncooked food, sat Pepito, looking very glum indeed. But Minimus' eyes brightened. Here was delicious-smelling food for a hungry dragon, for, when dragons are hungry, they are not very particular whether their food is cooked or not. So while Leah spoke to Pepito, Minimus scurried about the kitchen, smelling all the different spicy food.

'What is wrong, Pepito?' asked Leah.

'Ah, little one,' replied the sad Mexican, 'business, it has not been very good, and the man from the gas company came here a short while ago and cut off my gas cookers. I cannot make any food at all, and I will have to close down my restaurant.' Leah felt very sorry for him, and she knew that her father would be sorry too, because he often came to Pepito's for lunch.

'Is there nothing that can be done?' she asked.

'No,' replied Pepito, 'nothing at all. I am afraid I am finished.'

Of course, Minimus didn't hear any of this. He was too busy sniffing at all the different things you can smell in a

When the Dragon Lost His Fire

Mexican restaurant, and the more that he sniffed and snuffled the hungrier he became.

Finally he could control himself no longer and took a large mouthful of some small, thin, red and rather shrivelled fruit-like things in a basin on the bench. As he chewed and chewed, he felt a delicious warm sensation in his mouth that grew until the inside of his mouth was almost red-hot, and as he swallowed the curious red things, his throat and stomach became hotter and hotter as well. Soon all of his body felt as hot as a furnace and from deep inside his stomach came a rumbling, grumbling sound. Suddenly from his mouth came a large puff of smoke, followed by a roar and a burst of flame. Leah and Pepito turned around at the noise.

'Minimus!' cried Leah. 'You can breathe fire again!'

At the same time Pepito shouted, 'Hey, dragon! You have eaten all my chili peppers!'

Leah rushed over to Minimus, who had surprised himself as much as he had anyone else, and threw her arms around his neck. 'Oh Minimus, Minimus,' she said to the still-smoking dragon, 'you have got your fire back!'

Pepito could not understand what was going on, and was becoming a little annoyed that Leah was hugging and kissing the dragon instead of whacking him on the tail. But Leah was so happy that she led Minimus out of the kitchen and back to the table where her mother and father were sitting and wondering what all the commotion was about.

'Minimus is all right! Minimus is all right!' she said

delightedly. Pepito, who had followed her out of the kitchen, still could not understand what was going on, until the excitement died down and Leah's mother and father told him the whole sad story that now seemed to have a happy ending.

Then Pepito took Leah's father to one side, and told him about the trouble he had had, and before very long they had worked something out.

Every night for the rest of the week, Leah's father took Minimus out in the car in the early evening and returned home with him late at night. Leah did not know what was happening, and when she asked what her father was doing her mother said that he was just repaying a favour. At the end of the week, Leah's father took Leah along as well, and they went to Pepito's restaurant. They took Minimus into the kitchen, where Pepito had a large dish of chili peppers in a bowl on the floor. Minimus gobbled up the peppers greedily and within a moment or two was breathing great gouts of hot fire into Pepito's ovens. Pepito busily prepared food as Leah and her father went into the dining room, which was beginning to fill up with customers.

'Minimus is helping Pepito run his restaurant,' said Leah's father, 'because Pepito gave Minimus the means of getting his fire back. Pepito has had so many customers this week that he now has enough money to pay the gas company and they will reconnect his ovens tomorrow.'

'Is that what Mummy meant when she said that you were repaying a favour?' asked Leah.

When the Dragon Lost His Fire

'Yes,' he replied. 'Pepito was so pleased Minimus could help that he has let Minimus eat all the chili peppers he can for free.'

And in the kitchen Minimus breathed fire for the pleasure of it, and Pepito cooked tacos and tortillas and chili con carne, whistling a happy tune to himself.

The Watch Dragon

The Great Dog lay out on the warm concrete in front of the back door. But he was not asleep. He was distressed and worried. He had a cold. It was not a bad cold, nor was it a sneezing, coughing cold. Instead a snuffling cold; the sort of cold you get at the end of winter when the warm spring days start but the cold winter nights continue. His black, shiny nose, normally so reliable, was blocked and runny.

The Watch Dragon

The Great Dog, whose proper name was Aster Telperia, knew that the cold would go away in a few days, or a week at the longest. The Owners were giving him medicine twice a day, which was unpleasant, but Aster knew it was necessary.

Still, there was a very big problem. Because his nose was blocked and runny, he could not smell, and smell is most important for a dog. It is more important than seeing. Even if a dog is almost blind, if he can hear and smell he knows what is going on in the world around him.

Like all other dogs, Aster could not see colours. Everything he saw was like a black and white photograph with blacks and whites and many, many shades of grey. His nose told him much more than colours could. He could not see someone coming, but he knew someone was approaching if he could hear with his large, soft, sharp ears, and he could tell if the person was familiar or a stranger by scent. To a dog, the smell of anything is as distinctive and personal as a fingerprint. When it is dark, a dog does not need to see. His ears and nose tell him everything, and when he is asleep, his ears and nose are always alert. This is why, when a dog wakes up from a deep sleep, he is wide awake and ready.

Aster knew that because he could not smell properly, he had to rely on his eyes and his ears, and he was really worried because he could not do his job properly. He was a watchdog. He was not trained as one, but all dogs are watchdogs. This ability is something they are born with, something that has been with them since the First Dog came into the First Man's cave during a storm to warm himself before the Man's glowing, crackling fire and was given a bone to chew on. Ever since that time, dogs have repaid the debt for Man's kindness by keeping watch when Owners are asleep and unable to protect themselves, or if Owners are doing the things Owners do and are not paying attention to what is happening in the world around them.

Aster sniffed a wet, snuffly sniff and could smell nothing. What would happen if strangers came to the house? How could he tell if they were friends who should be greeted with a wagging tail, or strangers who should be barked at until the Owners came and spoke to them? And what of the strange, dark figures who crept around at night and went into people's houses by way of a window instead of a door, who never spoke to the people who lived in the houses but instead took money and jewellery and television sets without asking, and who caused great sadness in the house the next day? Aster knew of these things, for animals are great talkers who discuss everything that goes on around them, and people often do not know half what animals know. So it was that Aster Telperia, the Great Stripy Dog who looked after the Owners in the white house, was worried.

From behind him came the sound of a rustling and a soft footstep. He looked up and turned around. If his nose had been in proper working order he need not have done so, for he would have known at once who was coming. It was

Minimus, the little red dragon who lived in the house. Minimus didn't often come downstairs from Leah's room where he spend most of his time, but on this day the spring weather was so warm and fine that he didn't want to stay cooped up inside.

'Hullo, Aster,' said the dragon. 'How are you this afternoon?'

'Dod so good, Bidibus,' sniffed the dog. His nose was so blocked that he couldn't talk properly. 'I'b god a code.'

'So you have,' said Minimus sympathetically. Dragons don't get colds. Their fiery breath keeps their nostrils clear.

'Id's very bad,' said Aster, not stirring from where he lay on the concrete. 'I don't know whad I'b going to do.'

'I wish there was something I could do to help,' said Minimus. He was always helpful, but he knew nothing about colds and wasn't sure if there was anything he could do for the Great Dog who lay mournfully in front of him, his eyes heavy with worry.

'The Owders are trying dere best,' said Aster, 'ad dey are givinc me bedicine, which I can'd daste, I'b so stuvved ub. Id's brobably awful, adyway.' He sighed a long, heavy dog sigh that made his heavy dog lips go flop flop flop.

Minimus lay down beside him. 'If the owners are giving you medicine,' he said 'you will be better soon.'

'I suppose so,' said the dog, 'bud I can'd do whad I'b meandt to.'

'What's that?' asked the dragon.

'Keeb wodge over the Owders. Especially ad dighd.

Thad's whad dogs have to do, ad I car'd. I car'd smell a thing.'

'But you can see and hear,' said Minimus.

'If I can'd smell ad dighd, I'b almost useless and who knows whad might habben? Oh, dear.' Aster paused. 'I may led the whole family down.'

'But how?' asked the dragon.

'By dose dells be everything,' said the dog.

'Do you mean that you can smell someone at the gate before you even see him?' asked the dragon in amazement.

'Further,' said the dog. 'I cad sbell him od the street before he geds do the gate.'

'That is extraordinary,' said the dragon, and he was quiet for a while, thinking. Then an idea came to him. It was such a good idea that he became very excited and got up and jumped around because he was so pleased with it.

'Oh, Aster,' said the excited dragon, 'I know how I can help.'

'Really?' said the dog, and he cocked his ears so that he could listen carefully.

'It's simple,' said the dragon. 'I can see further than you can. I must be able to, because I can fly. My eyes are better than an eagle's.'

'Thad's dice,' said the dog, 'but how's thad goinc to helb?'

'We can work as a team!' exclaimed the dragon. 'Two of us can keep watch. I'll be your extra eyes and I'll tell you if anyone is coming. I'll fly up to the gable of the roof and

The Watch Dragon

from there I will be able to see all around for miles. If anyone comes I'll call out or blow a puff of smoke and then you can start barking and everything will be all right.'

'Thad sounds like a gread idea!' said the dog, and stood up and stretched. 'But I thing id would be bedder if you called oud. On a dark dighd I bighdn't see your sboke.'

'Let's give it a try,' said Minimus. He flew up to the gable at the top of the house and sat there as still as a stone and looking like a gargoyle.

'If I see anything,' he called, 'I shall call out to you and you can start barking. Why don't you lie down on the concrete again and wait?'

'All ride,' agreed the dog, and he lay down again and dozed. But he made sure his ears were on full alert for the sound of Minimus' voice.

Minimus sat on the gable and looked carefully around him. Below he could see the front gate with its white letter box and the front driveway with its large, white, wooden gates. He could see the garden with its trees and flowers and the garage at the back of the house where the Owners put their car. He could see the houses up the street, and the cars as they passed to and fro, and he could see, at the end of the street, a small group of shops. Over in the distance he could see a tall hill with a single tree growing from the top of it and a large park with paddocks where sheep grazed contentedly and new-born lambs gambolled in the warm spring afternoon. Next door, lying on the grass, he could see the strange black cat that was forever climbing to the top of the fence and looking at Aster. But the cat was curious, not sociable, and it never said a word.

Minimus' attention was attracted by the sound of a car slowing down. It was turning into the driveway of the house and stopping at the white gates. Now was his chance to put the plan into operation.

'Aster, Aster!' he called.

Aster was suddenly wide awake. He leaped to his feet and barked long and loud. There was a sound at the gate, but he couldn't smell a thing. But it had worked. Minimus had warned him that a stranger was coming, and here he was, doing his job. This was wonderful. It was perfect. It was . . .

The Lady Owner opened the gate.

'Aster, Aster,' she said comfortingly. 'It's only us,' and Aster saw Leah sitting in the car outside the gate. Of course. About this time the Lady Owner always came home with Leah, who had been at school. How embarrassing to bark at the Owner! It was shameful. A dog didn't bark at his Owner. It meant that the Owner was like a stranger, and that could never be.

The Lady Owner and Leah went into the house. Minimus fluttered down from the gable.

'You see?' he said, his dragon chest puffed out with pride. 'It worked.'

'Id was the Owder,' said Aster, humiliated. 'To keeb wodge you bust know the differedce bedween Owders ad their frieds ad stragers. You only bark ad stragers.'

'Oh,' said Minimus, somewhat downfallen.

The Watch Dragon

'Do you know the Owders and their friends?' asked the dog.

'Of course I know the Owners,' said Minimus, 'but I'm not too sure about their friends.'

'Oh, dear,' sighed Aster. 'I don'd thing this is goinc to work.'

'Don't give up Aster,' said the dragon. 'We must keep on trying.'

'I subbose so,' said the dog, 'but shall we leave it until night? Thad's when I will really deed some help, especially after the Owners have gone to sleep, or if they go out.'

'Yes,' said Minimus, 'I think that would be a better idea. If the owners go out, or when they go to bed, I shall fly up to the gable and keep watch.'

'Good,' said the dog, 'And . . . Bidibus . . .'

'Yes?' said the dragon.

'Thag you for tryink to helb me.' And Aster meant it.

That night, when the Owners had gone to bed, Minimus once again joined the Great Dog outside. The night was cold and the wind was rising. Black clouds scudded across the face of the waning moon.

When he had worked out the signals with Aster, Minimus flew up to the gable once again. He found that the wind had become quite strong and the air smelt of rain and a storm. Aster hated the rain, and went and sat in the door of his dog house. If he had to go out and get wet he would, but he refused to stand in the rain if it wasn't absolutely necessary.

The wind was no longer soughing through the trees, but

Dragon Smoke and Magic Song

was blowing the new green spring growth about quite violently. The sky became even blacker, although it was night, and the moon and stars could no longer be seen at all. Minimus had to grip the gable tightly with his dragon claws, for he was only small and rather light, and he was afraid that a strong gust would blow him off his perch. He looked down at Aster who was sitting patiently in his dog house.

Minimus noticed a car travelling slowly down the road. As it travelled, its lights went out. He thought that very strange, so he kept watching. The car stopped a short distance down the road from the white house and the driver got out. He was wearing black, and had it not been for the keen dragon eyes of Minimus he would have been very difficult to see indeed. But something else was strange; the man in black was carrying a sack over his shoulder. Minimus saw the man in black look about him furtively and suspiciously, then he crept carefully towards the white house. Minimus was shocked; the man looked as if he was up to no good.

Instead of going to the front gate, the man went around to one of the windows. *Aster will know what to do*, thought Minimus, and he called out to the dog. But the wind was too strong and the dragon's voice was too thin to carry over the rising storm, and Aster did not hear him. Minimus looked at the Great Dog, still sitting patiently in the door of his kennel. *Why doesn't he bark and run out?* thought the worried dragon.

The Watch Dragon

Minimus decided to leave his perch. As he flew off, he saw the man in black tinkering with one of the windows, prising it open with a metal object. Minimus sped down and flew past him; the dragon could not use his fire, for the house was wooden and he didn't want to cause any damage. The man could not have seen Minimus, for he kept on at his task. Minimus banked around the corner of the house and flew to Aster's kennel.

'Aster, quick!' he called. 'Something is very wrong.'

Aster leapt to his feet and started barking loudly. He was a very big dog indeed, and he had a great, booming, resounding bark to match his size. On this night, when Aster barked, the windows shook. Aster's bark was a deep, sonorous, frightening sound, and he raced around the side of the house. But the man in black had taken fright, and Aster could see him racing out the front gate and down the road. The dog was furious: this man had actually touched the Owner's house! He gave chase, his long legs speeding across the lawn and down onto the pavement. Minimus was in the air, keeping an eye on things. Below him was the man in black, running as fast as he could, and behind was Aster, giving chase; his bark had now changed to the howl dogs give when the hunt is up.

Then the storm broke! Lightning arced across the sky, bathing the surroundings in a ghastly white glare. The thunder roared in answer to Aster's howl and the rain poured in torrents from the heavy dark clouds. The wind roared up the street, driving the pounding rain ahead of it,

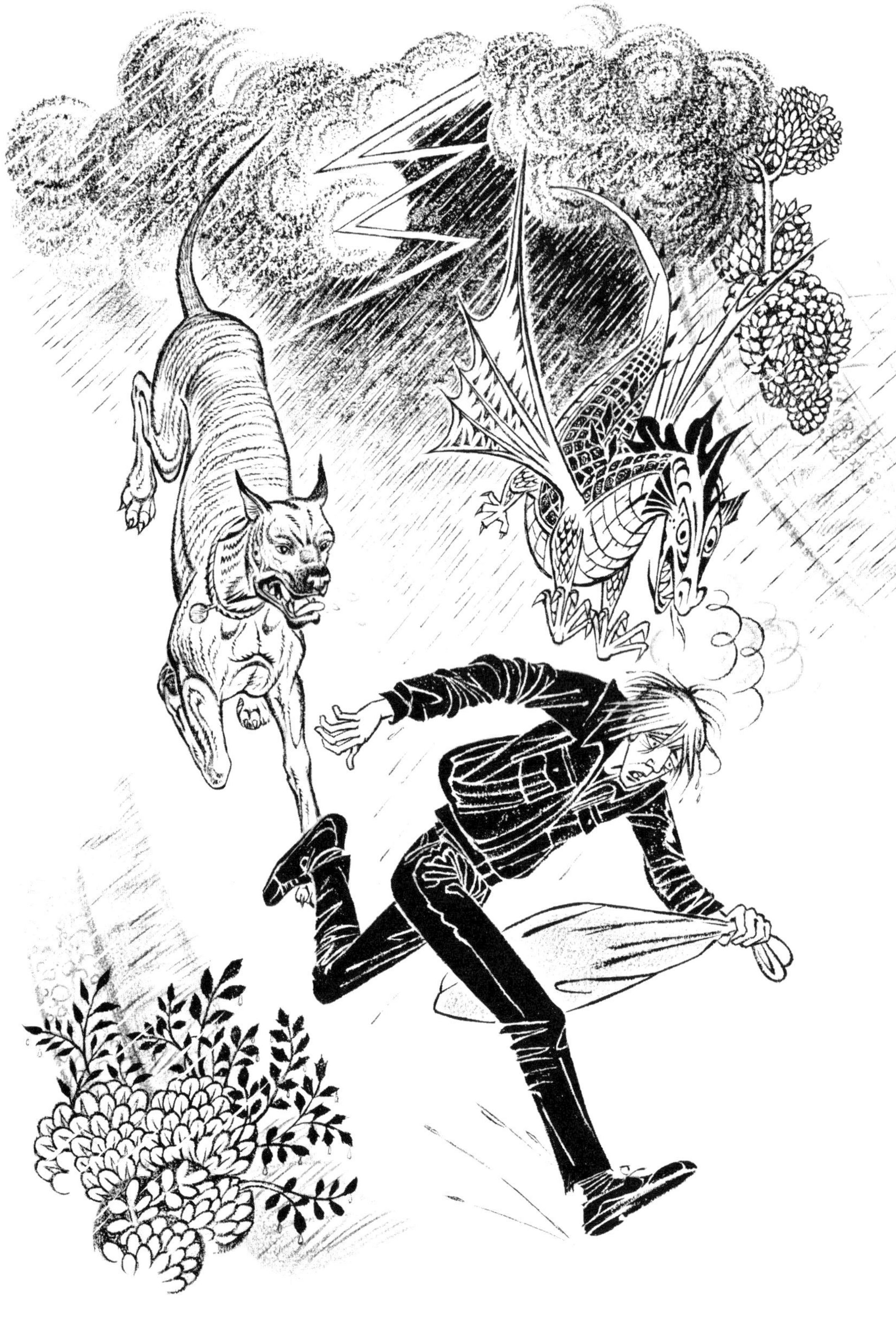

The Watch Dragon

and it buffeted the dragon fiercely. But Minimus was resolute. He had to help Aster, and he kept flying, even though the storm was at its height.

Aster did not notice the rain. He had to keep the man in sight. If he lost him, that would be the end; because of his cold and the rain that destroys scent, he would never catch him. Aster pounded on. He could not have believed that a man could run so fast. But the burglar had a great fear of Aster, and his fear gave speed to his feet. On and on he ran. He had no time to stop at his car. He had to get away from the huge dog chasing him.

Aster was breathing heavily now; his cold was taking its toll and he was becoming tired. But he could not stop, nor could he slow his pace for one step. He ignored his tiredness and the pain of his heavy breathing and ran on.

Up in the sky, Minimus flew on. He could not rest either, for if he had done so he would have been carried away by the howling wind. He could see that no matter how hard Aster tried, the man was gaining ground, for Aster was not a young dog. Aster had not stopped, nor had he taken a rest. Despite his age and his illness he kept up the chase, but Minimus could see that the man would get away if something was not done. He decided to take matters into his own dragon claws. He flew up, riding the wind to gain height, then, like a bullet, he sped down, down, and struck the running man.

The man did not know what had hit him. He tripped, slipped and fell heavily onto the road, and Minimus tumbled and rolled along the wet grass verge and into a nearby clump of bushes. Within seconds Aster was on the scene, panting, the foam of tiredness and effort around his muzzle, his tongue hanging out. But he still had the energy and the power to growl menacingly at the man, who lay on the ground, wet, miserable and frightened of the Great Dog who towered over him. Minimus scrambled out of the bushes and went over to Aster.

'Good work, Minimus,' said Aster, gasping for breath. 'If you hadn't tripped him like that, I don't think I would have caught him.'

To the prostrate burglar, this conversation sounded like strange growls and movements of the eyes and ears, because when they talk animals use more than just their voices. But to Minimus it meant even more than Aster said. From the way he spoke, it was clear that he was very tired indeed and needed help. The rain was still driving down and the wind was still blowing in great, heavy gusts. Minimus knew that Aster could not stand there indefinitely.

'I'll try and find some people to help,' said Minimus.

'Good idea,' said Aster, looking relieved. "I'll tell you what to do. There are men who help in this sort of situation. They wear blue uniforms and drive about in cars with blue flashing lights on the top. If you can lead one of those cars here, the men in it will take care of this one.'

Minimus wasn't quite sure what Aster meant, but he knew that he had to try. Once again he took off and up into the storm. He had to fly low to stay below the storm clouds and he kept his sharp eyes on the road. Many, many cars passed along the road, but not one of them had a blue flashing light on the top. Then he saw that pulled up outside a hamburger stand was just such a car. It must be the one! A man in a blue uniform was buying a hamburger and another was in the car. The car also had a large sign that read 'POLICE' and Minimus wondered why Aster failed to give him such an obvious clue. Probably, he thought, because the old dog was worn out with the chase.

The dragon swooped down low in front of the car. How could he make the men follow him? He landed on the bonnet of the car so he could think about it. As he did so, the man at the hamburger stand turned around.

'Hey!' he shouted, and his eyes went wide. The other man in the car peered through the wet windscreen and his jaw dropped in amazement. Minimus was frightened, leaped up into the air and started to fly down the road. As he did so, the man outside the car climbed into the driver's seat and followed the fleeing dragon, because policemen are always curious about things that are out of the ordinary.

Minimus looked behind him and saw the car following him. Of course! All he had to do was lead them to the scene, and so he flew low and slow, just fast enough and far enough ahead for the policemen to keep following him, and he led them to where Aster still kept guard over the wet, cold and frightened burglar.

Minimus flew out of sight behind a tree and Aster barked loudly to attract the policemen. But the policemen didn't need Aster's bark to stop them, for the burglar himself was calling out for help. As the policemen clambered out of their car, Aster quickly sought the shelter of a nearby tree. From there he could hear the burglar begging to be arrested and telling the police of his villainous activities. Aster smiled to himself. It was a job well done.

Minimus put his head around the tree trunk.

'Aster,' he whispered, 'can we go now?'

'Yes,' replied the dog, 'but we have a problem. I didn't keep track of how we got here. My nose is still blocked, but the rain will have washed away the scent anyway. I'm afraid we're lost.'

He hung his head in shame, sorrow and exhaustion. Minimus knew that if Aster didn't get home to his warm dog house very soon, he would be a very sick dog. The tree provided some shelter from the rain and Minimus told Aster to stay there. For the third time that night, he flew into the storm. He started to look for landmarks he had seen from his spot high on the gable end of the house. The night was too dark and the clouds too low for him to find the high hill with one tree on it, but one by one familiar landmarks became visible. He flew swiftly, checking the roads, and, sure enough, they led home.

He flew back to Aster. 'Do your feel well enough to follow me?' he asked the tired dog.

'I think so,' replied Aster, 'but don't go too fast.'

The Watch Dragon

So the dragon and the dog set off. Minimus flew a few metres ahead of Aster, and lit the way with bursts of fiery dragon breath so the dog could see. When they reached home, Aster crawled gratefully into his dog house, and fell into a deep and dreamless sleep. But Minimus did not sleep. All that night he kept watch over his friend.

The next day dawned bright and clear, with only a wet roadway and a few scattered leaves to bear witness to the storm of the night before. Aster was pleased that the weather was good and, as the fine spring days followed, he could feel his strength returning. Each night he slept soundly and Minimus kept watch at the gable end. As Aster began to feel better and better, he taught Minimus how dogs keep watch, and very soon Minimus knew all that there was to know about watching and guarding and warning.

Aster never forgot how Minimus had helped him on the night of the storm and one day he said to the dragon, 'I appoint you Watch Dragon of this house, Minimus, and I shall give you a watch name — you shall be named Stormrider in memory of the first night of your watch when you rode the winds and caught the stranger.'

Minimus was very pleased. He would have blushed except that he couldn't because he was already red.

'Have you got a watch name, Aster?' he asked.

'No,' said the dog, surprised. He had never thought of a watch name for himself.

'Then I shall give you one,' said Minimus, 'and I name

you Stormrunner for the way you ran through the wind and the rain and held the stranger.'

So it was that the dragon and the dog gave each other special names in memory of their great effort together. Aster smiled to himself. His cold was gone and he could smell again. All was well and he and the dragon would now work as a team, keeping watch over the Owners. After all, what more should a Watch Dog and a Watch Dragon do?

Aster and Minimus had many long happy evenings together, keeping watch. Never again did they have such an exciting adventure as they did on the night of the burglar and the storm, but peace and quiet were much better, and they had time to talk. They spoke of many things.

One night Minimus was in Leah's bedroom, checking to see that all was well before going down to join Aster who was standing outside, for the evening was warm and clear and the stars glimmered brightly in the sky. Aster was very old and his muzzle was quite white, although just around his large, black nose the fur was still jet black. He liked looking at the stars, for they made him feel young again, and he remembered the days when he had been a puppy. Although he looked back on those days with fond memories, he was still glad to be with his Owners, and to be the First Dog of the house, a position of great honour and responsibility.

As he looked at the stars, one glowed more and more brightly, until it made all the others shrink in size and brilliance. Aster was bathed in a clear, pure white light, and the light shimmered around him and was so bright that he had to screw up his eyes. From the centre of the light came a shape of a man. Aster did not bark, for he knew the man meant no harm, and that he had come to Aster himself. The man stepped out of the light. He was tall, and he wore a pure white robe, fastened at the waist with a belt of silver. On his shining golden hair was a band of silver and on the centre of the band, above his forehead was a great emerald. The man's face was beautiful. He smiled at Aster and Aster knew who he was.

'Hullo, Aster,' said the man. His voice was rich, deep and pleasant.

'Hail, Explorer,' said Aster.

'It is a pleasant evening, don't you think?' said the Explorer.

'Yes, indeed,' said Aster.

'I am about to set out on a voyage,' said the Explorer, 'and I need a good and faithful companion. I have been told that of all dogs, you, Aster Telperia, Stormrunner, Great Heart, First Dog, are the best and most faithful.'

Aster started in surprise because the Explorer knew all his names.

'Aster,' said the Explorer, 'I should like you to come with me.'

Aster hesitated before he answered. He looked into the deep blue eyes of the Explorer. They were like the eyes of his Man Owner, and Aster saw love and kindness, caring and compassion. He knew he could not resist Explorer's request and that the time had come for him to make his great journey.

'Where are we going?' he asked, and the Explorer smiled.

'To the stars you love so dearly, and beyond the Gates of Forever to the Islands of the Golden Sun, where you may await the arrival of your Owners, who will come later.'

'I should like that,' said Aster, knowing that the bond between him and the Owners had dropped away. 'But first I must go and see the Owners and Minimus and say farewell.'

'Of course,' said the Explorer. 'I shall wait for you here.'

So Aster passed through the door and into the house and went up the stairs. Minimus was coming from Leah's room and he saw Aster at the top landing. Although he had a white muzzle, Aster looked younger. His coat was a glowing gold and brindle, and his eyes reflected the light of the stars. His ears were large and soft, his nose wet and healthy. The years had fallen away from him, and he was young in spirit once again. As he stood before Minimus, he looked beautiful, tall, alert, proud and magnificent.

'Aster . . . er . . . what?' Minimus was struck dumb.

'Hullo, little dragon,' said Aster. His voice was deep, resounding and musical and it had a slight echo to it, as if he spoke from a far distant place.

'What are you doing here?' asked Minimus, 'I was just on my way down.'

'I have come to say goodbye,' said Aster, and he went into Leah's room.

The Watch Dragon

'Goodbye, little girl,' he said, looking at the peaceful head upon the pillow. He recalled the years they had spent together, remembering a time when the little girl had been much smaller and able to run between his great legs. He wished her the gift of love and left.

Leah stirred in her sleep. 'Bye, bye, Aster,' she mumbled sleepily, and the dog smiled to himself.

He went into the Owners' room, saw the Lady Owner sleeping quietly, and wished her love and peace. She smiled a reply in her sleep.

He walked around the bed to the Man Owner, gazed at his face and hesitated for a moment. Should he go? He must, but what would the Man Owner do? Of all the people in the house, the Man Owner was closest to Aster, who was a man's dog. Every day the Man Owner fed Aster and gave him water, spoke to him and scratched his ears in just the right place. The dog kept the Man Owner company while the Man worked at night, writing and thinking great thoughts. And the Man Owner spoke to the dog as an equal. How often had Aster wished he could reply in the Man's words!

Aster sent thoughts of love to the Man Owner and to the Lady Owner, telling them he would wait for them in the Island of the Golden Sun, beyond the Gates of Forever. Then he said goodbye.

The Man Owner called his name once and went into a troubled sleep, but Aster calmed him with a thought.

Minimus was waiting on the landing. 'Watch over them,' said the Great Dog, and softly glided downstairs. Minimus followed. He saw Aster go through the door and saw the Explorer outside. He knew at once that Aster was about to embark upon the last great journey, a journey that Minimus would make thousands of years later, and he went outside.

'Farewell, Stormrunner,' he said. The tears rolled down his scaly red cheeks as the Explorer put his hand upon Aster's noble head. Together they passed into the brilliant white pool of light and vanished.

Minimus flew to the gable end of the house and watched as a brilliant star gradually faded until it was just one of the billions of stars twinkling in the sky. That night and every night thereafter, Minimus kept watch alone.

The Lord of the North Spire

Jordis swung easily on the oars as the little boat rounded the point and headed out into the few hundred metres of channel between Solfin Promontory and the North Spire. Beyond the regular swirls caused by the tip of the oars and the turbulence from the stern of the boat, the waves rose easily and broke against the jagged rocks at the base of the cliffs. The cliffs rose high and dark and sheer and were topped with a sward of green. And beyond the thin line of grass the grey stone walls of Solfin Hold leaped upwards towards the sky, a manmade extension of the natural cliffs. The great, heavy eastern tower rammed upwards beyond the walls and was topped by two brilliant flags that fluttered side by side. The banner of the Lord of Solfin was deep blue with a single, many-rayed star at the top corner nearest the mast. And beside it was a deep red flag with a crouching golden lion in the centre. Above the lion was a gold crown, the banner of the Regent of Acquitannia, who was visiting the castle with his family.

On the seat at the stern of the boat, dressed in clothing the colour of which contrasted violently with the sombre, brooding darkness of the cliffs, sat a golden-haired boy. He was Melric, second son of the Regent and Jordis' companion on this expedition. Jordis pulled on the oars slowly. The row was not a long one, but the currents and tides that swirled through the channel were strong, and he had made the journey often enough to know that there was no sense in rushing and tiring himself out. Melric, on the other hand, was impatient.

'Can't you hurry, Jordis?' he demanded. 'I'm sure it wouldn't take me this long to row such a short distance.'

'We'll get there,' replied Jordis, and bent to his task.

Melric turned and looked back at the castle.

'It's a dour-looking place, 'he said, curling his lip disdainfully. 'I don't understand why you should want to live there.'

The Lord of the North Spire

'The Lord of Solfin, Jaiwain, is my uncle,' said Jordis, 'and my father Jareth sent me to Solfin to learn the ways of knighthood. I had no choice in the matter. I just did as I was told. But I don't regret it.'

'I couldn't live there,' said Melric. 'Give me Chineron or London any day.'

'You go where your father tells you, in the same way as I do,' said Jordis. 'Do you have a choice?'

'I suppose not,' replied Melric, and he smiled. 'How long have you been at Solfin?'

'I came to Solfin when I was eleven,' said Jordis, 'and now I am thirteen. Two years, perhaps a little less.'

'This is the first time I have accompanied my father on a progress,' said Melric proudly. 'I am thirteen, too, and already I have seen nearly all of Western Acquitannia.'

'What is the progress for?' asked Jordis, for all he knew was that the Regent was coming to visit, but he was not told the reason. Such things were not the business of boys.

'I don't really know,' said Melric, 'But I am sure it must be some important matter of state. I think father wants the support of the Lords for some enterprise or other, but I really don't know what it is. All I know is that he sits closeted in conference everywhere he goes. I know if he is successful, because then he is happy, but if things have gone against him, he rides alone and in silence, with rage about him like a cloud.'

'What do you do while he meets and talks?' asked Jordis.

'Not much,' replied Melric. 'Go out, play in the castle court, walk around town with one of father's clerks.'

'Do you find that dull?' asked Jordis.

'Oh, yes,' laughed Melric, 'That's why I took the chance to come with you, because it was different.' He paused. 'Come along, we haven't got all day.'

Jordis cast a glance over his shoulder. The North Spire was close now, and he could see the great arch which led into the sheltered bay. The North Spire was a curious rock, shaped like a triangle with the apex pointing north. Enclosed within was a bay to which entrance could be gained through the arch that opened through the rock's base. The bay was very sheltered and safe, protected from the wind by the crags and peaks around it. There was a single high crag at the apex, jutting about one hundred and fifty dizzying metres into the air. It was Jordis' private place. The people in the village of Solfin would not venture near it, saying it was a place of fear and magic, particularly when the fog swirled around the base of the rock at the time the Elder Folk gathered. If there had been any danger in the place Jaiwain would never have encouraged Jordis to go there. But the Lord of Solfin knew that boys needed a private place, and there were none in the castle. Jordis often came to the rock to fish, explore and dream and he frequently stayed overnight, safe within the shelter of the bay.

The archway entrance to the little bay within the North Spire was high and narrow and the current swirled on either side. But Jordis knew the place well and skilfully and swiftly rowed the boat between the rock pillars, using the currents, and they were within the bay. The water was smooth and calm and its surface was like a mirror, reflecting the walls of rock that surrounded it. Jordis guided the boat to the beach, and its keel scraped against the golden sand. Melric scrambled out on to the beach as Jordis pulled the boat up on the sand, and secured it with a rope to an old tree stump nearby.

'What a perfect place!' cried Melric, looking around him. 'Just perfect. You say no one comes here? That it is all yours?'

'I've never seen anyone here,' replied Jordis, but it is part of my uncle's fief. It is not mine.'

'He lets you use it, and lets you come here on your own. That's good enough.'

'There's a cave over here,' said Jordis, indicating the base of the towering Spire. 'When I come here for the night, this is where I stay. A fire at the mouth of the cave is all I need. Look, it's quite deep and dry, too, which is odd.'

'Truly wonderful!' said Melric, passing two great trees that grew either side of the mouth of the cave. 'And not too dark, either.' He went inside. 'The walls are quite smooth,' he observed.

'Yes,' said Jordis, 'and the end of the cave is, too. You might think the stone was dressed by a mason, for it doesn't appear to be natural.'

'How do you think that may be?' asked Melric.

'I don't know,' replied Jordis, 'but I asked my uncle what he knew of the place. He refused to talk about it. Said that I would learn in good time.'

Melric laughed. 'There is probably some deep magic

here,' he said, 'or perhaps it was a refuge for pirates or the men of the Raven Ships.'

Jordis became serious. 'There have never been pirates off the coast of Solfin, and as for the men of the Raven Ships, we prefer not to joke about them.'

'Come, now,' said Melric gaily. 'I was in jest.'

'Even so,' said Jordis, 'the men of the Raven Ships harried these coasts for many years. They sacked and plundered and pillaged and caused great misery until my ancestor Brinbora, who was a Lord of Solfin, mustered the people and took them out in ships where they met the men from the North in their Raven Ships before they could land. There was a mighty sea battle, or so the bards say, and the waters were crimson, and many brave men became food for the fishes and the sea birds. But the men of the North were beaten, and their wives and children and old folk tremble at the name of Solfin and they come here no more.'

'You say that like a bard,' said Melric quietly.

'Thank you,' said Jordis graciously, 'but I have heard the story often enough. It is one well-loved by bards in this part of Acquitannia. Brinbora built his ships in Haven Bay. The shipyards are still there, but they do not often build long ships there now.'

'We saw the shipyards as we came to Solfin,' said Melric, 'but I didn't know how they got started.'

'Now you do,' said Jordis.

Melric looked around. 'What is there to do now? You are Lord of this rock, Jordis. Show the son of the Regent your domain.'

The Lord of the North Spire

Melric was a proud boy, proud of his good looks, proud of his father, the single most powerful man in Acquitannia, proud of his rank and not a little vain about his appearance. He was dressed in a rich ruby velvet doublet, shot through with threads of gold, colourful hose and soft leather shoes. He wore a cap that matched his doublet upon his head and beneath it flowed his long golden hair, a feature common to all his family. Now he imitated his father, pretending that he was the visiting Lord, demanding that he be shown over a vassal's lands.

'There is not much to see,' said Jordis, 'and you are not dressed for climbing.'

'I can climb,' Melric said. 'And it matters not how I am dressed. Let us climb to the top of the Spire so we can survey all that lies below.'

'Are you sure?' said Jordis. 'There's a track to the top of the Spire, but it is steep and rough and ill-formed.'

'I need no track,' replied Melric loudly. 'I can climb any cliff. What is at the top?'

'That track stops short of the top, and I have not been to the highest pinnacle,' replied Jordis.

'Why not?' demanded Melric.

'Because there's a sea eagle nest there, and I will not disturb it.'

'Even better!' cried Melric. 'We shall climb to the top of the Spire, and I shall return with a sea eagle feather in my cap!'

Jordis thought for moment. He didn't like the prospect of taking the son of the Regent on what could be a long and dangerous climb. Suppose something happened. Suppose Melric tripped and fell and hurt himself — or worse. It would be his fault. But then he thought again. He knew the path, rough and rugged though it was, and had climbed it on his own many times. He was sure he could guide Melric as long as the golden youth curbed his impatience. And as for the sea eagle nest, he would deal with that when they got to the top.

'Very well,' said Jordis. 'But you must follow me, and put your feet where I put my feet. Be careful, and don't rush.'

Melric stared at Jordis for a moment. The boy from the West had a tone in his voice that spoke of command, and an assurance in his manner that seemed beyond his years.

'It shall be as you say,' answered Melric. 'Lead on.'

The path was easy at the start, and wound gradually up from the beach. On earlier visits Jordis had cut or enlarged holes for steps and hand holds and they made light work of the first hundred metres. Jordis paused for a rest and looked upwards.

'It isn't so easy from here,' he said, 'but you can see where the path runs up through the rocks. It is narrow and tricky, but if you follow me closely we will be quite safe.'

Melric was slightly out of breath, but he did not tell Jordis. He could not have the other thinking that he was so used to the soft life of the cities that he could not comfortably climb the towering rock. Jordis climbed up further, carefully making sure he did not send any loose stones down on Melric who was following him. Once they were through the defile, they stopped again. The path ran along the top of a ridge that led to the base of a large pillar of rock that was the top of the Spire.

'This is where the path is most treacherous,' said Jordis, 'for the ridge slopes steeply on either side of the path, as you can see. If you should slip, you would not stop until you hit the water. Are you sure you want to continue?'

Melric took the question as a challenge. He was out of breath, and the palms of his hands were grazed and roughened. His colourful hose had torn where he had scraped his legs against rocks, but he would not stop now, nor would he turn back.

'Let us continue,' he said.

'In a moment,' said Jordis, 'for I want to get my breath back.'

Melric looked towards the top of the Spire. On an outcrop a couple of metres above the end of the path, was a mass of twigs and sticks — the nest of the sea eagle, cunningly built in such a way that it was sheltered from the cruel winds that swept around the high place. That was where he would get the feather for his cap and flaunt it in the same way as his father wore a sprig of yellow broom flower.

After a few minutes, they started the last leg of the climb. Jordis was right, thought Melric, as he scrambled, half walking, half crawling, carefully following Jordis' steps. The ridge sloped sharply to the edge of high cliffs on either side. On the one hand was the open ocean, the powerful sea rolling below and crashing against the foot of the cliffs.

On the other was the still bay, but the drop was just as steep. Those who dwell in castles and walk the battlements or climb the narrow circular staircases to the top of the watch towers have little fear of heights. Even so, Melric was glad there was no wind and that the day was still.

Jordis had reached the base of the rock pillar and extended his hand to help Melric over the last few metres. They sat together in the warm sun and looked around them. To the south, and over the channel loomed the great bulk of Solfin Hold with its two powerful keeps and tall watch towers. High as they were, they could see that the great Eastern Tower was even higher. Melric was astounded. He did not know that Solfin Hold was quite so vast and imposing. Certainly, it could be seen from a great distance, but, high though they were, and in such a wild and open place, the Hold was higher and greater than it seemed from the landward side. Melric looked out over the ocean towards the west.

'What lies over the ocean?' he asked.

'Have you not heard the tales of the Western Sea? asked Jordis.

'No,' replied Melric.

'No one knows what lies over the ocean, but it is said that beyond the Western Horizon lie the islands of Lyonessia, a fabled land where men have never ventured, or if they have, they have not returned. And even beyond that, is the Reef of the Edge of the World and the Pillars of Sunset, and the Islands of the Golden Sun.'

'Old wives' tales,' scoffed Melric.

'If you think the Elder Folk are old wives, you do yourself disservice and them great insult,' snapped Jordis.

'Surely you don't believe in those things,' said Melric.

'Why not?' asked Jordis. 'No man has sailed so far West and returned to say yea or nay to the tales. But the Elder Folk have recounted them in their wisdom, and the Teachers do not deny that there are lands beyond, where man may not tread. Whom am I to dispute with the Teachers?'

Melric could see that further arguement was fruitless. He was rested now after the climb.

'The eagle's nest is above us,' he said, looking upwards. 'I think I may just be able to scramble up there and get my feather.'

'Be careful,' warned Jordis, 'for this is the time when the eagles have chicks. Take your feather, but do not touch any eggs, if there are eggs there.'

'All right, all right,' said Melric impatiently. 'Can you give me a leg up?'

Jordis cupped his hands and braced himself against the base of the rock pillar. Melric placed his foot in Jordis' cupped hands and scrambled upwards.

'Can you see anything?' asked Jordis.

'Yes,' replied Melric, 'I've got a feather; it's a beauty. And there are some eggs in the nest. Do you want to see one? I'll bring one down.'

'No!' said Jordis angrily. 'I told you not to touch any eggs. Leave them there.'

Melric paused. 'Oh, very well. Let me down now.'

Jordis lowered his hands and Melric landed on the ground beside him. In his hand was a large brown feather with a bright white tip.

'Look,' he said. 'Isn't is magnificent?' And he admired his prize. *It is indeed a good feather,* thought Jordis, *and it will look good in his cap.*

As they looked at the tail feather of the sea eagle, a shadow crossed the sun, blocking out the bright light. The two boys looked up. Above them, wheeling in the open sky, swiftly returning to its nest, was a sea eagle, the lord of the open coastal skies in the West. Jordis shivered momentarily.

'I think we should not be here,' he said. 'If there are eggs in that nest, as you say, the eagle will do all it can to protect them.'

Ascar the sea eagle had been flying in the warm morning sun, looking for food. His mate was far out to sea, following the fish shoals, but he knew he could safely leave the nest and its eggs for the hour or two that he would be away. The warm sun would keep the eggs comfortable.

But now, as he returned, he was aghast and angered at what he saw. Two young men were near the nesting place. His rage grew within him as he saw the two figures start to interfere with the nest. His fury was kindled by his instinct to protect the nest, the territory around it, and most importantly, the eggs that gave promise of new, young sea eagles.

He wheeled upwards to gain height, screaming his fury to the sky and sea. In his scream was the wrath of sea eagles, which is a mighty thing to behold. It is said to be so great that they once challenged the storms of evil sent to assail them and tear them from their place on the edge of the sea and sky. Ascar dropped out of the sky like a stone, without fear, the air rushing through his pinions. He had a single purpose — to dislodge the intruders from the rock.

For an instant, Jordis could see all that was going to happen, and through his mind flashed all the possible results of the sea eagle's descent. For a moment it was as if he was in the mind of the great bird as it streaked like a bolt of lightning across the clear sky and down towards them. He could see both himself and Melric, their arms and legs flailing helplessly, falling, falling down the side of the North Spire and on to the sharp, cruel rocks below. He could feel the merciless tearing of the great talons raking across his face and down his arms, tearing his young flesh to the bone. He could feel the pain, and the fear, and the sorrow of his father and his uncle, and the anger of the Regent Hemric when the news was taken to them.

He could not allow these things to happen. He moved, wrapping one arm around the body of Melric and half ran, half crawled along the narrow ridge from the base of the pillar to the defile below. Perhaps if he could reach the safety of the higher rocks that would surround them in the defile and get away from their exposed position, the attack of the sea eagle would be frustrated. But to remain where they were was to court an inevitable end.

Melric said nothing. Despite his previous confidence, he

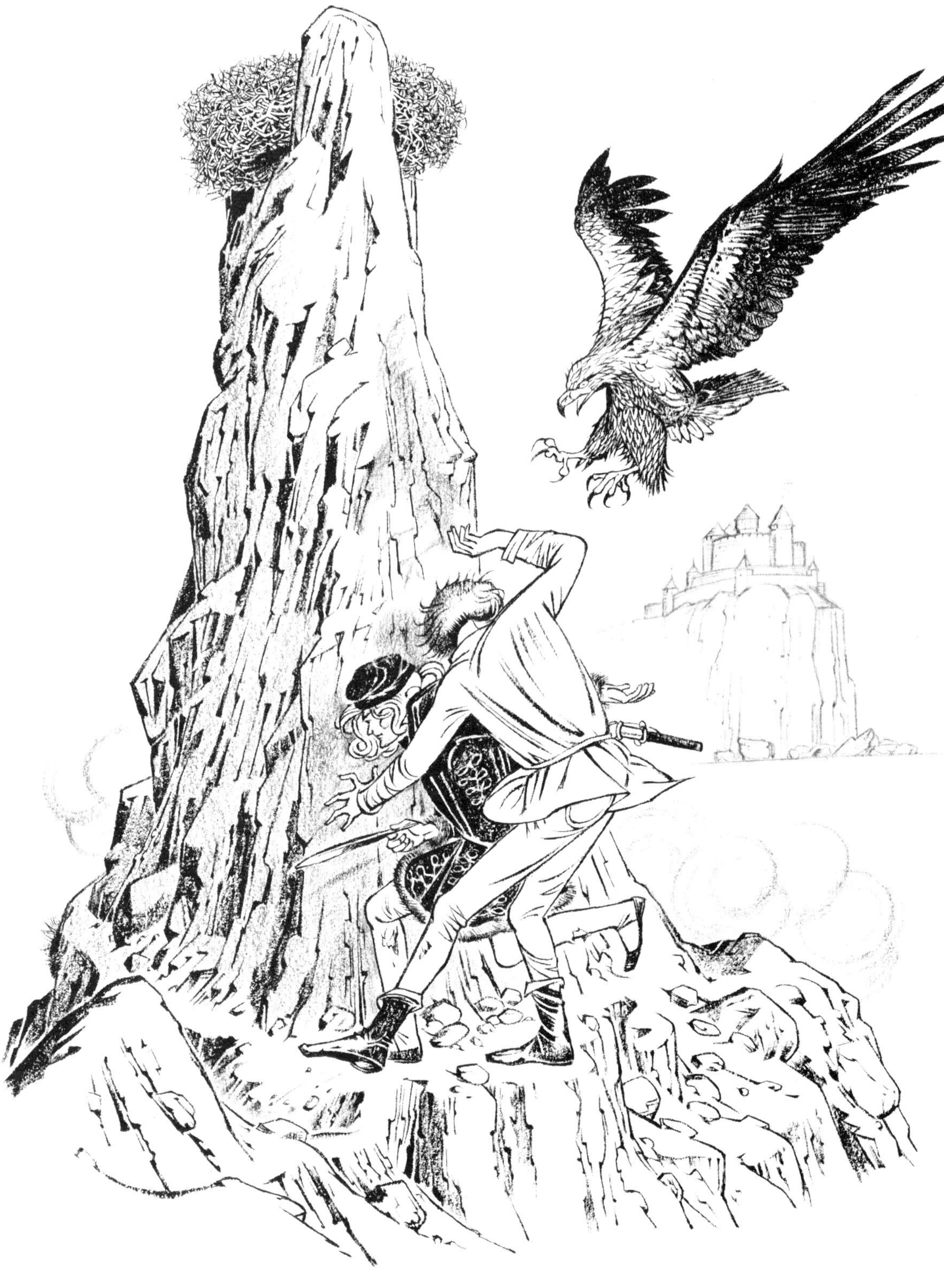

The Lord of the North Spire

was now afraid, and he trusted himself to the boy who knew his way about this fearful place.

Loose rocks and stones slopped beneath Jordis' feet, cascading down the sides of the ridge and over the edge and down the precipice to the rocks and the sea below. He could hear the sea eagle screaming its defiance at them as it came ever closer. The defile seemed to be a long way away as Jordis scrambled and shoved and slopped and tumbled. Miraculously he held the path, and, only a few metres away from the mouth of the defile, pushed Melric forward and down so that the golden-haired youth, his cap awry and his gorgeous clothes dirty and torn, tumbled into the safety of the high rocks.

Jordis turned, and as he did so, Ascar was upon him. Ascar struck at Jordis in the same way that he struck at fish lying just beneath the surface of the water — fast and hard — relying upon his power and the shock of his impact to stun the boy. But Jordis was no fish, and he caught the power of the eagle's strike upon his upraised arm. The long, sharp points of the eagle's talons tore through the sleeve of his jerkin and bit into Jordis' arm. Jordis toppled backwards and into the safety of the defile, and Ascar lost his grip, though he tore three mightly gouges in Jordis' arm. Blood began to soak the tattered sleeve of Jordis' jerkin, but he scrambled to his feet, calling to Melric to go further down and out of danger. Jordis would face the eagle; Melric had to be kept safe and away from the fury of the bird.

Ascar wheeled upwards again, gaining height for another attack. Jordis saw Melric moving quickly through the defile and downwards towards the protected track. Jordis moved further into the defile and the shadow of the bird was above him, screeching in frustration, unable to fly into the narrow passage and inflict further harm. Ascar circled over the defile as Jordis followed Melric down and on to the path, and together the boys reached the safety of the beach. As they felt the sand crunch beneath their feet they heard a cry far above the, not a cry of anger, or the war cry of the sea eagle, but a cry of anguish.

What the two boys now saw before them caused them to stop in their tracks and forget the harsh and frightening events that had just happened. Over by their boat, sitting on the gunwales, was a figure clad in a long robe of a creamy colour, wearing a cloak of dark brown. In one gnarled hand the figure held a long wooden staff, and the other hand, which rested on his knee, was gloved; an ornate leather glove, embossed in gold. From beneath the cloak protruded the pommel of a sword.

The man raised his face and looked at the boys with piercing blue eyes that glittered beneath bushy white eyebrow. The man's face was framed by long, grey hair, and he had a long and magnificent grey beard. His eyes seemed to penetrate the boys, and they both felt that he could see into their minds; they could feel him within their souls.

The man stood up and walked over to them. It seemed to Jordis that his feet only just touched the ground, and that his form was surrounded by a golden glow that shimmered as he walked. As the man approached, the boys were surprised to see that, although he looked old at first glance and had the marks of age in the texture of his hands and the colour of his hair, his face was smooth and his eyes were young.

The man stopped a few paces away from them and rested upon his staff. For a few moments he said nothing and the boys were too shocked to utter a word. How had he come. There was no sign of another boat. Had he been there all along? If so, where did he stay? Jordis was more surprised than Melric. He had been there many times and had never seen another soul on the North Spire.

Then the man spoke. His voice was rich and his accent was unfamiliar, though he spoke the Common Speech. The sound of his voice was as deep music, old and magnificent and beautiful to hear, and it soothed the boys' fear and anxiety.

'So you have met Ascar?' said the man.

'Who is Ascar?' asked Jordis. His voice trembled and sounded small and insignificant to him against the melodious tones of the man before him.

'Ascar is above you,' said the man pointing towards the sky with his staff. Above them, high in the sky, the boys could see the soaring shape of the sea eagle.

'We meant no harm,' said Jordis.

'No,' said Melric, and his voice and the edge of fear. 'We only climbed up for a look at the Spire and at the eagle's nest.'

'Ascar doesn't like strangers,' said the man, 'and if his

mate Averar had been on the nest, you would not have been allowed to approach as close as you did. The sea eagles are lords here and are jealous of their high places.'

'We meant no harm,' repeated Jordis, and he was angry at himself. Was that all he could say to this imposing person?

'I am sure *you* did not,' said the man. Melric shifted uncomfortably.

'I think you should meet Ascar,' said the man, a faint smile creasing his lips.

'I have already done so,' said Jordis, and he raised his arm which was aching from his wounds.

'Let me see,' said the man. With his ungloved hand he rolled up Jordis' sleeve, and his firm but gentle fingers examined the wounds. 'You are a brave one to face the wrath of the sea eagle,' he said. 'Not many would do so.'

'I didn't exactly face him,' said Jordis, and smiled grimly. 'It was more to allow Melric to get to safety.'

'Yet you did not use your knife,' said the man, indicating the short dirk at Jordis' belt and that all young men in Acquitannia carry.

'No,' replied Jordis, wincing slightly as the man probed further.

'It is good,' said the man softly. He reached beneath his cloak and into the folds of his robe. He took out a small jar, and from it smeared salve upon his fingers and rubbed the slippery substance into Jordis' wounds. Jordis could feel warmth run through his arm, and the pain began to fade.

The Lord of the North Spire

'That will give you some relief,' said the man, 'and will help to heal the wounds. You will have scars, I am sorry to say, but they are scars of honour and of courage. Now you must meet Ascar, for he has unfinished business.'

He pursed his lips, and gave a call that was like a whistle and like the cry of an eagle, and he raised his gloved hand. From the clear sky above, Ascar came down, down. Jordis admired the power and the beauty and the magnificence of the bird, and wondered at this man who seemed to command it with such ease. Ascar flew into the bay, skimmed along the surface of the water, revelling in flight as only birds can and fluttered to a stop perching on the outstretched gloved hand of the tall man before them.

'This is Ascar,' said the man.

The bird looked at Jordis with yellow eyes. Jordis could see no sign of fear nor of hatred in them and admired the beauty of the sea eagle, standing proudly and arrogantly upon the hand of the man. Ascar's head was covered with pure white feathers, and the feathers of his body and wings were a golden brown that glistened in the sun. His long, brown tail feathers were tipped with white.

Then Ascar looked at Melric, and his expression changed. His eyes narrowed, and from his long, hooked beak he gave a cry of anger and anguish. Melric returned the eagle's look.

'You have something he wants,' said the man.

'What?' said Melric, haughtily.

'Don't bandy words with me, boy,' said the man. There

was a ring of anger to his voice, and his eyes grew cold. 'You have something that belongs to Ascar. Give it back to him or the consequences may be dire. You forget you are in the presence of the lord of this place.' From the way he spoke, Jordis could not be sure if the man referred to himself or to Ascar.

Melric's eyes became fearful. He reached into his doublet and withdrew his hand, in which he held a small object.

'Hold out your hand,' said the man. Melric did so and Jordis was horrified to see that on the palm rested the egg of a sea eagle. Jordis was furious. So that way why Ascar was crying in such a way! Didn't this town popinjay know the danger he courted in stealing the egg of a sea eagle? It was amazing that Ascar had not attacked them on the beach; he would certainly have made their trip across the channel to Solfin Hook a bad one had he attacked them. The bird would never have given up the chase. Jordis cursed the stupidity of the son of the Regent. Why hadn't he heeded Jordis' warning?

'Calm yourself, Jordis,' said the man. His voice was even more soothing than before, and Jordis forgot his anger.

Ascar flew off the gloved hand, and hovered above the egg. Carefully, with one talon, the mighty bird gently took the egg, enclosed it in his powerful claws and gave a cry of joy. The man whistled once. Ascar flew in a circle around his head, still crying joyfully, and soared upwards.

'He will go to his nest now,' said the man. 'It is well for you that the egg was not broken, otherwise Ascar would have exacted a weregild, and I can tell you in all truth that the price would be high, and I could have done nothing to prevent him.'

'Who are you?' asked Jordis.

'Who am I?' asked the man in reply, and he laughed softly. 'I am of this place and of many others. I am here, and I am there,' and he pointed in the direction of the land.

'Are you a teacher?' asked Jordis.

'Some say that,' replied the man.

Now Melric spoke, and his voice had the sound of regret for his folly and arrogance. 'You are of the Elder Folk,' he said.

'No, I am not *of* them, but I am near to them. I shall say no more, except that I am a Protector. More you shall learn later, especially you, Jordis, for I shall see you again. As for you, Melric, you have much to learn, but I think now that you are on the path. Remember that it is not enough to be a Regent's son to command respect. By your actions and attitudes shall you win it, and I can say that in the future you will. Both you and Jordis will spend some time on the same road together. Now I must go. You will stay here until I do so, and although you will remember this day, of its events will be able to say nothing. Such is my decree, save for one thing. You may speak of it privately together.'

He turned, and seemed to walk across the beach and towards the mouth of the cave. The great trees on either side of the entrance seemed to bend momentarily as if in homage as the man passed. Then the cave filled with a blinding light which grew and grew and faded as quickly as it had come. As it did so, Jordis and Melric found that they could move again. The pain in Jordis' arm had vanished, and the wounds were beginning to heal.

'Never again will I scoff at old wives' tales,' said Melric, and he laughed. 'And I still have my feather.' He indicated the sea eagle feather in his cap. 'I'm hungry. Let's go home.'

And so Melric and Jordis went back to Solfin Hold in the boat. This time Melric rowed, for he was grateful to Jordis for what the boy had done to help him in a time of trouble. In later days they would talk together of the adventure on the North Spire, but mysteriously to others they could say nothing. But it is said that when they rowed back across the channel, with the golden-haired boy on the oars, merry and laughing, and Jordis enjoying the good companionship, there could be seen shepherding them back to shore, a mighty sea eagle that circled low over them as they rounded the point, and flew, high and proud, back to its nest on the North Spire.

Ngarara the Taniwha

One fine summer's day, when the sun shone brilliantly upon the foliage of the forest trees and glittered on the surface of a large lake in the middle of the mountains, Ngarara the taniwha lay in the cool water, his great head resting on the warm, white pumice sand of the beach. Suddenly the forest fell quiet. Not a sound could be heard. The song of the birds was stilled. The screech and scratch of the small insects stopped. It was as if some great event were about to happen.

Ngarara opened one great dark eye and then the other, and looked around. All he could see were the sand and the brilliant greens of the leaves of the forest, shining in the sun. As he watched, from the forest fluttered a small fantail. The bird flew quickly to Ngarara, and perched on his rough, horny head beside his ear.

'What is it, little one?' asked the taniwha. He was old and wise and he had an idea what the answer might be.

'Greatest and Eldest,' said the fantail politely, 'Man is in the forest and is coming to the lake.'

'So it has happened at last,' sighed Ngarara, and thought for a moment. 'We have all heard of Man, but he has never been here before. Spread the word through the forest, little messenger,' he said to the fantail, 'and let all the creatures know of this news and bid them be careful.'

'What will you do, Eldest?' asked the fantail.

'I shall go to the depths of the lake, and think upon this thing,' replied the taniwha. As the fantail flew off, Ngarara swam swiftly to the deep water, and dived deep, and lay on the bottom, thinking and waiting.

Julia and Jason Forsythe were children who were on a camping expedition with their father John, who was a naturalist — a man who studied plants and animals and how they lived together. Every summer, John would take Jason and Julia on expeditions so they could learn about the beauties and wonders of the world around them. This

Ngarara the Taniwha

trip was special, because they were exploring in the mountains which were large, unmapped and dangerous. But John was careful, and knew what he was about. They had carefully marked their path into the forest so they would know their way out; they had plenty of food, good camping equipment and warm clothing.

It was Julia, Jason and John to whom the fantail referred when he took his news to Ngarara.

Julia was the first to see the lake.

'Look Daddy!' she said, 'A lake! Isn't it beautiful?'

'It is,' said her father. 'I wonder what it's called?'

They walked quickly to the beach and looked around.

'This is magnificent,' said John. 'I don't think anyone has been here for a very long time, if ever. There certainly isn't any litter, or any signs that people have been here. You know, we could be the first people to see this place.'

Jason and Julia were very excited at that thought. John spread out a map upon which was marked a red line showing the direction in which they had been travelling. He looked carefully at the map, puzzled and concerned.

'I can't find this lake on the map at all,' he said, 'but I'm sure it should be just about here.' He pointed to a place on the map with his finger.

Together they studied the map, checking and rechecking. Finally, John said, 'I think we've discovered a new lake, kids. These mountains have never been explored thoroughly, and I guess no one has been here before. That would explain why the lake isn't on the map.'

'So what do we do?' asked Jason.

Dragon Smoke and Magic Song

'What do you think we should do?' replied his father, because he believed that children should try and think for themselves.

'Explore,' said Julia. 'Find out as much as we can, write it all down and report on it when we get back.'

'Right,' said her father, 'but before we start we had better set up camp.'

They found a small clearing near the edge of the lake, pitched their tents and scouted around until they had found some rocks which they took to the camp site. With the rocks they built a fireplace for cooking and boiling water because they all knew that it was not safe to drink water straight from a lake. When the camp was ready, they decided to explore the beach. Jason took a camera, John a notebook and the map and Julia used her eyes, pointing out things of interest. By the end of the day they were tired and hungry, but still excited by their discoveries. They cooked a meal and, as the sun set, went to bed for the night.

Every bird, beast and insect had watched their movements carefully and, after the sun went down, gathered at the edge of the lake to talk about the new visitors. As the moon came up, Ngarara the taniwha emerged from the depths of the lake and came to the meeting. When he heard what had happened, and what the Men had done, he was confused. These people seemed different from those the Moas had told him about many years before when they came to drink at the waters of the lake. But the Moas had been great talkers, inclined to exaggerate. These Men

Ngarara the Taniwha

seemed different from those of whom the animals had spoken, Men who fought fiercely with one another, and of whom the ducks and birds had spoken, Men who carried sticks that made loud noises and spat death.

These Men seemed careful about what they did. They did not destroy or break or kill. This was something that required even more thought. Even with his great wisdom, Ngarara could not fathom what he had heard about these Men, compared with the other news that he had heard about Men over the years. So, when the meeting ended, Ngarara retired once again to the depths to think and think some more.

Very early the next morning, as the sun was just beginning to glow faintly in the east, Julia awoke. She felt very thirsty. Half asleep, she got out of her sleeping bag and, without thinking, went down to the edge of the lake, cupped her hands and drank two mouthfuls of water. She felt better, went back to her tent and dozed off to sleep. A little while later she awoke, hearing voices.

'These Men are very lazy,' she heard one of the voices say.

'Aren't they?' came the reply.

'They are missing the best part of the day.'

'I know. They can't be very wise.'

'I wonder what the Eldest would think.'

Julia rubbed her eyes. Was she still asleep? She pinched herself. Yes, she was awake. Who could be talking? They had seen no one the day before. Could there be people outside? What did they mean, when they said 'Men'? Who was 'the Eldest'? Her curiosity overcame her as the voices continued. Quickly she slipped on her clothes and went outside. Her father and Jason were still asleep, and there was no one to be seen, except for a tui and a fantail, sitting on the branch of a tree.

'Look,' said the fantail to the tui. 'One of them is awake.'

'Yes,' said the tui, 'I wonder what she is going to do? Let's watch.'

Julia was speechless for a moment. She could understand what the birds said! But she didn't stop to think about it for very long. These birds were very cheeky.

'What do you mean, "one of them"?' she said. The sounds that came from her lips were not words, but the trills and twitters of a bird. Now it was the turn of the tui and the fantail to be amazed.

'She speaks! She understands!' they cried, and they flew off.

'Wait, come back!' cried Julia, but the two birds had gone.

She could not understand what had happened, but if she had spoken to Ngarara the taniwha she would have known. The lake was a magic one. All lakes with taniwhas in them were magic. But this lake had a special magic. Anyone who drank of the pure water of the lake could understand the language of animals, as well as their own. The power had to be renewed every few days or else it wore off. Julia didn't know about all this, and the more she thought about her talk with the birds, the more confused she became.

Ngarara the Taniwha

When they awoke, she tried to explain what had happened to her father and brother. But it was no use. Very kindly, and with some understanding for her concern and growing distress, they tried to tell her that she must have been dreaming. As they spent the day exploring, she continued to hear the comments of the birds and wanted to answer them back. She even tried once or twice, but her father and brother thought that she was just doing bird calls, so she gave up. It was very frustrating, because she knew that she could learn so much about the forest from the birds. But the thing that confused her most was the constant talk about 'the Eldest'. Although she couldn't imagine who the birds were talking about, she determined to find out who 'the Eldest' was.

That evening, when the day's exploring had come to an end, and Jason and her father had put out the light in their tent, Julia got up and walked to the water's edge. The moon was high in the sky, casting beams of silver over the water. At the edge of the lake she could see the fantail and the tui.

'Good evening,' she said, unable to think of anything else to say.

'Good evening, Julia,' the two birds replied.

'I'm sorry I haven't spoken to you very much today,' she said, 'but the others don't believe I can.'

'That's all right', said the tui. 'We suppose that it must be difficult if others don't believe the truth.'

'Yes, it is,' said Julia miserably. 'There is so much that we could learn from each other.'

'We already know much about Man,' said the fantail, 'and to be frank, we don't like what we know. Man cuts down the forests, kills the animals and birds for sport, poisons the waters and creates havoc wherever he goes. But I must be fair. You and your Men are different, and you treat the forest with respect.'

'Not all men are wasters,' said Julia.

'Nmmph!' snorted the tui. 'The ones we have seen are.'

At that moment a cloud scudded across the moon. There was a disturbance on the surface of the water, and Julia heard a swishing sucking sound from the lake.

'That was not a kind thing to say to a child, little tui,' said a deep voice from the darkness.

Julia gasped in fright.

'Who is there?' she said, her voice trembling.

'It is the Eldest, Ngarara the taniwha,' whispered the fantail.

'Yes, it is I, Ngarara,' said the taniwha, 'The birds told the insects, and the insects told the fish, and the fish came to me in my cave deep at the bottom of the lake that the girl child had drunk from the lake, and could speak the speech of the forest. Have no fear, little one,' he said to Julia, 'for Ngarara the taniwha would speak with you, and know your thoughts.'

'I cannot see you,' said Julia. 'Where are you?'

'I am here at the water's edge,' said Ngarara, 'But I warn you — you may find my appearance frightening. I am very large and very old.'

Ngarara the Taniwha

Julia walked down to the edge of the lake, where she could see, in the dim light, a vast, dark shape. The clouds fled from the face of the moon and she could see more clearly. There, in front of her, was Ngarara's huge head. On his face were huge ridges and whorls like *moko* – the face tattoos of the Maoris. The pupils of his eyes were as black as pitch, but she could see around them a rich gold colour. His large mouth was shut, but she could see the points of his mighty teeth protruding between his lips. His long neck was covered with great spiny ridges and the rest of his huge bulk which loomed behind him was covered in dark green scales. But there was a softness in his eyes and a calmness in his speech that belied his appearance, and Julia knew that she had nothing to fear.

'Are you really a taniwha?' she asked.

'Yes, I am,' replied Ngarara, and he chuckled to himself.

'I thought that taniwhas were make-believe,' she said.

'I am here,' said Ngarara. 'You can touch me if you like.'

So she did.

'So now I have been touched by Man,' sighed Ngarara.

'Is that so bad?' said Julia.

'No, I suppose not. But I have heard of the doings of Man, and what I have heard over these many, many years does not make me happy.'

'Is that why you are called 'Eldest'?' asked Julia.

'I am called Eldest because that is what I am. I can remember the days when the trees were very small, and I heard the great, grinding rumbles of the volcanoes as they erupted, changing the shape of the earth, making the ground shake and creating storms and tempests in the sky. I can remember the days when there were many taniwhas living up and down the land. I can remember the great talkers of the forests, the Moas, before they went away, never to return. I have heard of the arrival of Man to these lands, and how he killed the Moas, and his fellow Men. Oh, yes, I have a great and long memory. But now, in these later days, I believe that there are no more taniwhas, and that I am the only one left. The forest has grown about me, the birds and animals have come and gone and changed as the seasons. But I, Ngarara the taniwha, still remain, the last of my race.'

'Poor taniwha,' said Julia sympathetically.

'But I am not here to share my grief with you,' said Ngarara. 'I wish to know about Man. Would you sit with me and tell me what you know?'

'I'm afraid there isn't much,' said Julia. 'My father knows much more.'

'But he has not drunk of the pure water of the lake,' said the taniwha. 'Besides, from the mouths of children one hears truth, so speak on.'

So for many hours Julia sat by the edge of the lake, talking with the old taniwha. He asked many, many questions. Some of them were difficult to answer, but she did her best. Ngarara listened patiently and carefully to her answers and thought about what he had heard. Finally he said.'

'Truly, Man is a strange creature. I am not sure that I understand all I have heard, but I believe you have told

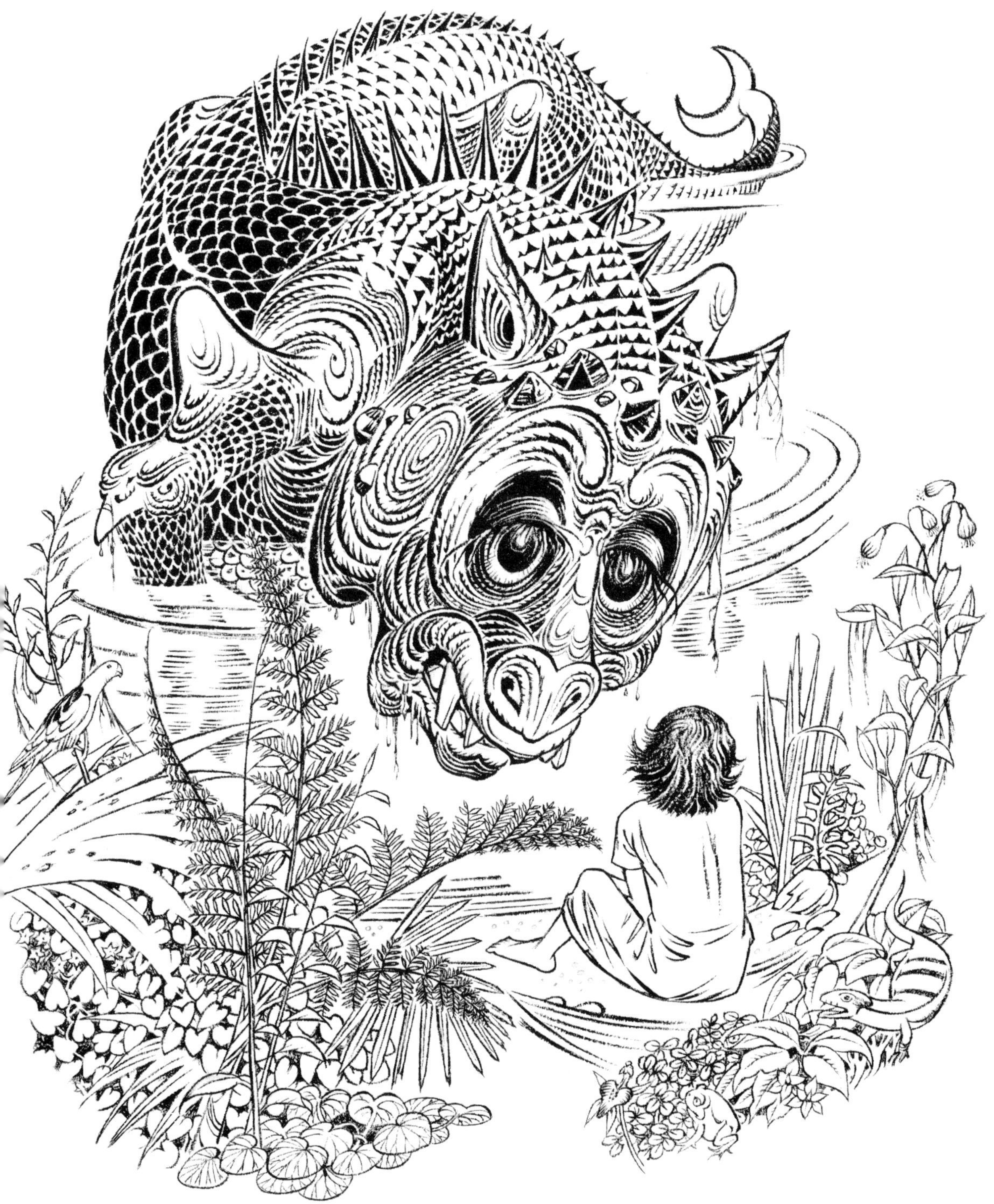

me what you can. And it is only fair that you ask me questions.'

For many more hours, Julia questioned the old taniwha and he told her many things that neither she nor any other person could have known. He told her of the beginning of Time and of the days before the Sun shone upon the earth, he told her of the shaping and gouging of the Land, of the coming of the first creatures and birds and of the growth of the forest. He told her of long summer days without number and freezing winter nights without end; he told more of the Great Moas, the storytellers of the bush, and of the stately Huia, the Lords of the Forest; of how the kiwi lost his power of flight and why the fantail flits and darts among the trees and ferns, of why the wood pigeon is so greedy and how the tui gained his tuft of feathers on his neck; of why the kakapo booms for its mate and how the morepork can foretell the weather. He told her of the beauty and delicacy of the forest and the life within it, and how everyone and everything depended upon everything else.

They talked and talked and they had not finished when the sky was touched a faint pink by the rising sun and dawn announced a new day. The birds became concerned and implored the taniwha to return to the depths of the lake. But Ngarara would have none of it. He wished to stay and meet John and Jason when they woke up, and wake up they did. They quickly discovered that Julia was not in her tent and immediately went to the edge of their lake.

Ngarara the Taniwha

Imagine their surprise when they saw Julia, small and pale in her nightdress, sitting on the edge of the lake and talking to a creature that was different from anything they had seen before. Julia turned and saw them.

'Come over here,' she called, 'and meet Ngarara the taniwha.'

As if in a dream, John and Jason walked to the water's edge and the taniwha loomed above them. Julia was talking to the taniwha, making sounds that neither her father nor her brother could understand.

'Don't you see,' said Julia, 'I can talk to him. We have been talking all night, and he has told me so much about things that we should all know. If you drink from the lake, you can understand too.' Like a torrent, the words flowed from her mouth, and the taniwha smiled to himself, for he knew of the excitement of children. Even the children of the creatures of the forest were the same.

He turned his head to John and looked at him with his deep dark eyes. John reached out his hand and laid it on the head of the huge monster. It was as if he had a complete understanding of what had to be done, but he thought for a moment. Again he looked into the eyes of the taniwha and saw that within the depths of his soul, the taniwha was seeking trust and friendship.

Then John spoke. 'Tell Ngarara the taniwha that we are very honoured to meet him. Tell him that we respect his land and his lake and his great age and wisdom. And tell him that we shall keep his secret.'

Julia looked at her father, not able to understand, but she did as she was told and repeated what her father had said to the taniwha.

'Tell the Man that he is a good person of high honour and that he knows the customs of the Land of Ngarara. Tell him that I trust him, and that I know that the secret of this place will be kept safe. And now, little one, I must say farewell. It has been a great meeting. I am glad that I have spoken with Man in peace, and have had a chance to share things with him. Farewell, little Julia.'

With that he turned, and swam away from the shore, and disappeared beneath the surface of the lake.

Julia repeated Ngarara's last words to her father, and then began to cry. John walked to her and put his arm around her shoulder and hugged her to him.

'Now we have met a taniwha,' said John. 'We are very lucky, kids. Taniwha were a part of the rich mythology of the Maori people, but now, for us, the legend has come to life, although it is said that the Maoris knew the taniwha well. There is a problem, though, and we shall have to make a decision.'

'What is that?' asked Julia.

'When we return home, we must not tell anyone about this. If we did, and we were not believed, they would think we were mad. And if we *were* believed, Ngarara would not be safe. He would be hunted and studied and the peace of his home would be destroyed. That is why I made the promise I did.'

Ngarara the Taniwha

His children agreed, although they were disappointed that they could not tell their friends at school. But they realised that Ngarara's protection and his trust in them were more important.

That very day, they struck camp and began the long trek back to park headquarters, where they had left their car. And when they got home, they didn't say a word about the lake to anyone. Julia's power of speech with animals and birds wore off, but not before she had told her dog and cat of what she had seen. Both pets were not surprised. They already knew of Ngarara, because animals are great gossips and even they have their secrets from Man. But they were pleased that Julia could talk with them, even if only for a little while.

As for Ngarara the taniwha, Eldest, he still lives in the lake and watches as the world passes by. He looks forward to the summer, when the sun is high in the sky, and three people come out of the bush, drink of the waters of the lake, and talk with him for many days. And his secret is safe with them.